$3.00

THE
HOOK
OF
IT
IS

BASIL
PAPADIMOS

EMERGENCY PRESS

Thanks to Ian McLachlan, Klee,
the referees at Le Strip, the old l'Esplanade crew,
and to Gill, who kept it all.

The author wishes to acknowledge the assistance of
the Explorations Program of the Canada Council.

Cover Photo of Katerina by Panayiotis Pantazidis
Cover and Book Design by Graphique PaleoStrata/Montréal

Published by Emergency Press
RR1 Enismore, Ontario. K0L 1T0 CANADA

ISBN 0-919740-03-0

Distributed by Les Editions de la Ruelle
695 Place du Parc , Montréal, Qué. H2W 2P3 CANADA
For a copy of our complete catalogue
please write to the above address.

Imprimerie Gagné Ltée - Louiseville, Québec

This book is a work of fiction. Any resemblance the characters herein
may have to persons living or dead is purely coincidental.

First printing

Printed in Québec

For Big Jay and Little J.

1

✈

Me and Stein are hanging out on the fried chicken corner at Queen and Augusta. Slouched against the pole, under the big, slow turning bucket. Frenzied Queen Street afternoon hustles past us, all fangs and credit cards, trampling any wino or half-wit who gets in the way.

Stein's looking east down Queen toward Spadina Avenue. His loose-lipped mouth slung open, bulging gray eyes way off to the vanishing point, breaking only for the office skirt or so that comes by. It's dead hot, early summer. Thick, sour air on the skin, sun perched on the forehead.

It's been almost two months since I came back from London. Fuck all. Had trouble honing in on the *rools* cool. Every action getting dated the same minute. When I took off to England last fall I thought things might work out but it was one more cold flop count-your-goddamn-pennies cheap scheme. Mouldy old island full of broken hearts and bad teeth. Might as well have spent the winter in Oshawa.

Loitering on Queen again now. Pitching the gimmick I picked up in the U.K. Wearing it through this heat wave. Trying to throw a scare into any hard, analytical head. Occasionally using cockney most people won't get.

So I'm standing on this fried chicken corner with a loser called Stein, remembering the time we met during breakfast at Rooneem's Bakery, a few days after I had gotten back from London. First thing he'd ever said to me: "I used to be a big wheel in this town."

Stein'd been sitting there, drinking coffee with a cackling, hawk-nosed bastard he'd introduced as the Duke. Whatever Stein was yammering about this other guy just laughed at, made fun of. Didn't bother Stein though, he'd just smiled and kept talking. In fact, he wouldn't shut up. Told me he'd been almost everywhere and knew everybody and everybody knew him. Said I looked like I was on the ball and he had this master plan he couldn't talk about but I should stick around. So I did. And today, seven weeks back in Toronto, I'm standing here in this bright noise wondering what the fuck.

☿

Stein pulls his eyes off the women going by and turns to me. Defeated, leathery mug. Matted brown hair, graying, receding. Thirty-two going on fifty. Bound up in ragged jeans, a green, sweat-stained polyester shirt. He pulls at the sleeve of my bike jacket, starts walking towards Spadina Avenue.

We straggle along this busy shack street. Go past a withered old Polack peering out a dusty shop window, one hand on his neck, counting his ailments, squinting up at those glass towers closing in.

Stein hangs a left into the Cameron Pub. It's daytime unlit, empty. Only an ancient, scar-faced Scot sits near the door swilling draft and talking to himself. The bartender doesn't look up from his paper.

Giving me a look, Stein goes for the can in the rear. We lock ourselves in the stall. Mixing speedballs with a Social

2

Insurance card, he's taking his time, sifting and working. "Man," I yell at him, "what you doing, reading your fortune? Just lay it out."

"I'm putting a little aside for later," he replies. "There's not much left. We should wait till we get a fit."

"Who gives a shit? Just hurry up."

Both of us snort up a couple thin lines. Stein returns the reserve supply to his sock. I lick the card and slide it into my back pocket. Coming out of the can we want some cheap beers but the Cameron's depressing during the day, quiet as a grave. Only at night this joint picks up, juke box blasting, bands in the backroom. Hair and leather hags crowding in, playing up for the tourists. At night the lights come on.

So thinking about a different kind of place to drink Stein says we ought to go over to the Legion Hall near the Rivoli Bar.

"They're war veterans," he tells me with a knowing frown. "They been through it."

We make our way down there sticking close to store fronts and buildings, staying in their narrow angle of shade. Eager to join those piss-stink reptiles with tin medals and bad memories, listen to their long-odds.

Get held up at the door by this thick fingered goon. "Too young," he says, "get lost. What war did you two fight in, anyway?"

"Fuck you, man," Stein's shouting at the guy. "Dieppe was a breeze, you shithead. We did ten years in Troy!"

"Where? Troy? What, the joint in upstate New York?"

"No, you moron! The war!"

Bloated old pigs going in an out stop to listen, side with their doorman. "Everythin awright, Jerry?"

Hand gestures calm. "Yeah, yeah..." Jerry the doorman is confused. "Okay, you guys," he gruffs at us. "It's only vets here. For old boys, y'know, your grandfather's age."

Stein's in a half-stoned panic, taking everything

3

personally. Bewildered rage, veins popping in his neck, temples. "What? My grandfather?! My grandfather never came to this hole!"

Jerry looks at me pissed off, wants me to drag this nutcase away, tell him what it's all about. Jerry's pork-chop face saying to me: *He's your buddy, you must know what's wrong with him. Take him away and fill him in.*

No, sorry, Jer. I wanna watch you deal with this headache. I got his leash right here but I'm not feeling too positive, you know, Jerry? I'm nearly flat broke and these pleasant people with their sunglasses walking by make me sick.

Jerry sees all this. His belly hair pressed up against the white acrylic shirt sees all this. Even his fat hands at his sides see all this. Nobody's that stupid, except for Stein.

I pull him away. "C'mon, forget it..."

Stein's still at Jerry. "You're finished, man. I know where you live."

Jerry waves him off and goes back inside.

"Fuckin nut..."

I drag Stein down the block a ways east, past the Baboon Club. Under the heat, through gangs of shopping addicts. Trend leech boutique owners stand in their doorways, salivating, darting eyes watching for teen-aged shoplifters. Car horns colliding, fevers running. Top dollar art chicks with tight lips and edgy haircuts rush past on some kind of mission. They only look to have you look so they can look away.

Wander over to the sidewalk hippie market at the corner of Soho Street, just by the Black Bull Hotel. All these industrious little Canadians pushing hand painted t-shirts, dogskin belts, scrap-iron jewellery, ripped-off afro-headgear. Unleashing the entrepreneurial spirit, working the magic of the self-employed. Recounting every cent with their nervous claws.

"Bunch of lousy hippies," Stein croaks. "Look at those

4

women...filthy feet. Christ, no shoes in the city. That's not holistic."

Hollywood Jobbers used to be here and a book store. Couple of frayed, run down places. The old Jews who ran Hollywood would sit on this sidewalk in kitchen chairs talking about I dunno what, saying hello and getting mad if you smoked in their store. They got torn down. Them and their kitchen chairs and their cheap coffee-maker and their tin roof and their no-smoking signs.

Story was some real-estate pimps from H.K. bought the land and were gonna build an office/retail/condo complex. Now it was a parking lot for awhile till they greased the Cakes at Queen's Park and Metro Council. Rumour said big heroin money was going through the wash, coming up clean as the Queen's complexion.

Me and Stein crouch on a couple plastic milk crates, sit there amongst the gleeful street vendors, watching their spiel and I am amazed, lord. There's Winnie and Minnie, those two vestal virgins. Can't beat them for bargain chic, they caught on right off. Rode in a few years ago from a pig farm out Peterborough way and now they're on Queen Street West and, man, they'd say they're doing just fine. There's Carrot-top selling her homemade frocks. Airheads hawking tie-dyed boxer shorts. Artist civil-servants come by, dead ahead severely all-black, zipper cut angles, more rigor than brains. They give us the know-better face.

"Wadda you lookin at, bull's-eye?" I yell at them. They ignore us, continue the crisp march to that on-the-dot appointment.

"Fashion pukes..." Stein grumbles and spits onto his third-hand dress shoes. Snatches up a piece of newspaper drifting past, goes to work on a polish. Makes me look down at myself. Crusty black Levis letting out a damp waft, the surplus cop boots already falling apart. Feeling the cramp in my guts. I'm watching Stein put the elbow grease to his shoes as the Duke strolls up.

5

"Hiya doing, guys?" he grins. "Tired out from shoppin?"

"What's going on?" I ask him.

"Dick all," replies the Duke. "Fronted a couple dimes from that ape, Danny, at the Project."

His fingers pull through the thinning blonde hair. The narrow, pointed face pans around, nods at some twirp nearby.

"You oughta know better," says Stein, shaking his head. "That Project shit is sprayed, full of PCP."

"Oh yeah?" answers the Duke with some spite. "What are you, Stein, a fuckin purist?"

Stein gripes to himself, goes back to his shoes.

The Duke stares down at me, still parked on the crate. A cheesy crease around his eyes. The rangy good looks fading into years of living off the stick. Lost his fashion sense a few girlfriends ago. Now he hardly gets out of the hand-me-over pants and steel-toed work shoes. Lives with the nagging doubt that thinking like a white man ain't what it used to be.

"Saw your wife a few minutes ago," he jibes me.

"She's not my wife," I rasp. "Leave her alone, she's not so bad."

Stein comes-to. "Then why don't you take care of her?" he yells into my ear.

"Stein, why don't you fuck yourself?"

He won't let up. Leans closer, pointing at me. "She's a good woman, Nick. You never appreciated her. You shoulda looked after her."

"Yeah, yeah...shut up already."

"C'mon, Stein," says the Duke. "You the family counsellor? Why don't you iron yur shirt sometime?"

"I don't give a shit about that," Stein snarls. "You guys, you're like the rest of them. You, Duke... Princess this, princess that. She's gotta have the clean ankle, perfect tits, right bit of leg. I'm no bourgeois fuck like you guys. I'm a

Marxist, ugly women don't bother me."

"That's clear enough," the Duke grunts, tired laugh. "Considerin you were plowing that diesel dyke, I see what you mean. What's her name, anyway?"

"Yeah, Stein," I poke at him. "What is her name?"

"What do you care?" he scowls at us. "Leave her outa this, she never did nothin to you. She's always polite around you two, gives yu both the benefit. Fuck knows, nobody else does."

"Alright, okay," groans the Duke, putting up a lazy hand. "We gonna do somethin or what?"

Stein's up on his feet, walking already. "C'mon," he says, "let's go back to Augusta."

Back to the room he graduated into. From park bench, from abandoned car, from doorstep. The backshed rickety dive on Augusta Street, just north of Queen. House of psychos, balding mohawks, skinheads with assholes tattooed on their foreheads, the dyke. Stein stuck onto the place like dry snot. Insinuated his way in. Dark room in back behind the kitchen. Always running out of money and dope but every time we're leaving he pulls another slice of tin-foil out of his shoe. And we'll hold hard there, loyal stickmen with a 24hr. caseload. Blasted right through a jackhammer morning, remembering to catch the breakfast special deadline at Rooneem's Bakery, chatting up the whitetrash cook. And she'd make a real nice breakfast but we're lepers to her and her Farrah Flip hair.

"Shit. You guys look like shit."

The Baltic drip who owns this caf doles out the creamers one at a time, praying for the moment the land values double. Laughs along with our backhanded chatter.

"Don't sit near the window, eh fellas? Do me a favour."

Working, news reading, smells-so-fresh one comes in for the early low-cal lunch. Turned out reborn from Hazelton Lanes, she's outgrown wearing the black widow gear. Gilt-edged burgundy talons picking at the cucumber

7

slices. She rapid scans the R.O.B., studies the Nikkei index for a moment.

"A wife like that, that's the way to go," says the Duke, his mouth feeling its way around burnt toast. "Like her," he points with his chin. "Not bad lookin, nice clothes. Probably has a little car, some cozy pad. A shot of brandy at night. You know, no bullshit."

Stein looks on at her while listening to the Duke's play-by-play. He's daydreaming on her, a box of cereal. Read the back. It says here she's just right. You get three chances, see, and it's only a matter of collecting five of her wrappers, then you send them away. It's easy.

"Sure," Stein agrees, "women are good when you wanna go home and just be quiet and watch them doing the things they do." These are the most secret secrets of our secret society.

She looks up at us for a second, our faces adrift in her sense of self. Three ragweeds bobbing on a small raft at sea in her. One bucket and a deck of smokes between us.

So give us the time of day at least, will yu, lady? Give us your money and charms and pictures of you as a small girl. Birthday party shots. Let us stand in the background with paper hats on and cake in our hands. Gathered round the dining room table, watching you blow out the candles. Your mother leaning down between us, lipstick razor teeth, pearls at her throat, holding the big knife.

2

♣

"Oh, Lord, it ain't easy..."

Tuning in with another American preacher wired through a Buffalo AM station begging for any amount you can possibly spare to help this ministry carry out its service to our lord, the baybee Jeezus...

"If man descended from apes, then how come there's apes around tuday, huh? You ansa me that!"

❊

Knock on the door downstairs.
Loud knock probably waking up this blue-stocking landlady of mine. Had all her hair removed years ago. I mean everything but her head and her cunt. You know, no fuss, no muss. Perfect pussy patch manicured into a clean triangle. But now she says she don't feel normal, skin problems coming up all the time. Too dry, rashes, brown skid marks here and there.

I know it's Chops at the door. He's this mouthy little barnacle who latched onto our crew at a speak a few weeks ago. Now he's showing up here at 3 a.m. to buy my time, prove he's on the mark. We'll sit in my tiny upstairs

9

kitchen jabbering until dawn, making the big plan. Chops'll wanna crash on the couch. The landlady will get pissed off, issue another warning.

I go down to get the door. When I open up Chops is bent over trying to see through the mail slot.

"What the hell you doin?"

"Lemme in. It's fucking cold."

"Where you been?" I whisper.

He gives me a wide-eyed look. "Well, I'm here now."

"Sh..."

We creep along the dark hall and up the stairs, creaking like an old ship. Landlady's rodent snout must have smelt Chops coming in. Lying in her bed, eyes popping open, assuring herself of her rights. I'm already hearing her sick whine about people who get up early and people who work and how she could get twice as much rent and I'd be out in the gutter if she wasn't such a saint.

I'm reheating the coffee and Chops is cutting coke on a fashion mag he pulls out of the bathroom. He keeps his ratty black suit jacket on, the jacket on top of two shirts and constant scarf. Pale, sagging baby-face bent close, mumbling something, talking to the girl on the cover. His green vein hands cutting the powder right on her eyes. She smiles at him all perfect teeth and pretty shade of lipstick.

"You gotta spike?" Chops asks over his shoulder.

"It's sorta barbed," I answer, taking it from a drawer and handing it to him.

He checks it out like a government appointed expert. "No," he decides, "it's fucked."

"How much you got left of Shank's quarter?" I ask him.

"Fuck Shank," Chops replies, face over the table top again. "I'll pay him, I turned over on this. He can wait." He swivels around at me, his mouth already open. "You know, Nick, I ran into Debbie the other day and, I tell you, man, she looked bad."

"Yeah?" *Who's Debbie?*

"Yeah. She was such a piece when I was screwin her. Now she's gone all soft. You know, jello butt, her tits are way down...it happens to women. Men just get older, they just get older and it don't matter. You marry a woman, y'know, and one day you wake up and somethin is growin outa her face."

He starts pulling the lines across the magazine with his Stanley knife. Now the cover girl's got white fence posts on her cheeks. She suddenly looks made up African.

"It's true," I nod. "Imagine being married to Sue."

"Sue?"

"You know, Rowski's wife. What an old pooch she turned out. And that baby she had, what a freak."

Chops is laughing and I'm rolling up a two dollar bill. Queen goes rolling by, scowling. I've got my face lined up when the hairless landlady pokes into the kitchen. Chops quickly pockets the bag. She glares at us, her cop heart measuring every pulse.

"I'm sorry, Nick, but it's late. I wish you and your friend could do this somewhere else."

"Where?" Chops hates her, believing she hates him.

Landlady stares at him, her mouth becoming pinched, sickened. Her hand reaches up and carefully touches some small white rags tied into her hair.

"Like your place," she says slowly, precisely.

"What if I don't have a place?" Chops mocks her, half a laugh gurgling out of him.

The landlady's icy calculator eyes widen, light up. She's provoked, wrath of the taxpayer on our necks. Get the leg irons. Where's the babyee Jeezus now?

"It's okay," I tell her, "we'll keep it down."

She's clutching the bathrobe, that synthetic sky blue thing she kept from the days when she'd never seen *Elle*. Fist gripping her together at the chest. "No!" she snaps at me, "I don't want this guy in my house."

11

"He pays the rent!" Chops yells. "This is his room, right here. You can't say who or what's in here!"

"Stop shouting!" she barks at him. "I own this house and I can say who comes in. You don't pay the rent."

They both look at me.

"Stop bickering," I say. "Go to bed, we'll shut up."

She takes it worse than Chops. To him this is a glorious victory. *Yeah, yeah, sure. We'll shut up, whatever you like, just get lost.*

"No! I don't want this guy in my house!"

I stand up, pulling Chops to his feet. "Let's go."

Landlady follows us down the narrow stairs telling me I don't need friends like this. She stands in the dark front door, arms crossed, watches us move along the dead street. Empty working week night, cold June twilight and I'm stuck with this toad-faced jack-off.

"You fuckin idiot!" I'm bawling at him. "All she wanted was for us to keep it down and she woulda gone back to bed. Fuck, man, you're so stupid."

"What is she, Nick, yur mother?"

"Fuck you."

"Relax. You just take too much shit, that's all."

"Yeah, too much shit...Let's go over to Stein's place."

"Are you serious?" Chops is sulking. "Stein's a bloody vacuum cleaner."

"So what? You got any better ideas, asswipe? We coulda stayed at my place if you weren't such a loudmouth."

Stein is already nodding that greedy head, hears our steps echoing down. Our thin moonlight shadows slide over the rows of tiny immigrant gardens down Palmerston, darken the doorways of hovels along Robinson. An eye out for slow cruising cops. Two wiseguys looking for the baybee Jeezus.

Stein's leering at our arrival like the maitre d' in an empty restaurant. Rubbing those monkey paws together, he ushers us through the sunroom and into his musty, crowded little pit. Pushes a heap of clothes off the sinking bed and drags over a half-busted wooden chair. His pupils glimmer, mouth in an eager, rubbery smile.

"Cold out, eh, guys? C'mon in. How's it going, Chops?"

"Okay. Freaky weather, eh?"

"Chops woke up my landlady," I say, flopping onto the bare mattress. "Got us chased out by playin my lawyer."

Stein sides with Chops right away. Sits at his brown, pressboard desk, begins tapping with a pencil, his legs apart, the judicious scowl, a hand gripping his knee.

"Aw...she's a little narc," he starts. "It's not Chops' fault. She's got somethin up her ass. I saw her on the drag tonight around seven with her loaf of rye and special crackers and cheeseshop cheese. I say hi to her and she gives me that weasel nose and walks past. No class."

Chops warms his hands on this evidence and even undoes his jacket. "Fuckin right," he joins in. "This guy's nuts for livin there. That broad on my case all the time. I wouldn't take it. Not that kinda bullshit."

"It's only temporary," I say, "a few more days."

Stein laughs, keeps up our mutt'n'jeff. "You been sayin that since you got back from England, Nick."

"Yeah, I have. Chops, bring out the bag."

"You got somethin?" Stein feigns. "Maybe you can front me a little, eh, Chops?"

"I can get us off," he replies, enjoying his moment. "Maybe you got a fit, Stein?"

"Sure," Stein wags his head, jumping to his feet, "still wrapped." Rustling through his boxes of worthless memos to himself and then practically crawling into a desk drawer he comes up with a new orange-cap.

Chops digs a spoon out of his pocket and reaches for the glass of stale water next to the bed. Him and Stein quietly arguing about amounts, holding the bag up to the weak light of the desk lamp, tapping at the white powder in the corner.

3

✝

I run into the Duke on the south side of Queen, at the bottom of Markham Street. He's loafing through the early evening, browsing the sidewalk deals in front of a third hand junk shop, toying with a disembowelled camera from the fifty cent bin.

"Hey, Nico!" he sees me. "What's shakin? I was just by your place."

"I been up to the bungalow," I tell him. "Watched tv for an hour, they drove me nuts."

"So how are the old man and the old lady?"

"Y'know, still squabbling. Another head busting battle over who really paid for the car."

The Duke holds up the dead Brownie, squints at me through its cracked lens. "Don't take it so hard," he says. "Maybe they're still getting used to being Canadian."

I look at him, his face crouching behind the little black box. The rusty shutter snaps open then closed.

"After 30 years?" I ask.

"Nick, Nick, Nick," he sighs, tossing the camera back into the bin. "These things take time."

"Yeah, probably forever. Why did they come to this country?"

///////

14

We cross Queen through the backed-up traffic, almost getting run over by one of Mr. Dong's delivery wagons.

On the north side of the street, at the doors of the burnt-out cinema, a bag lady's on all fours searching for her eyeteeth. A few ass-picking greaseballs lean against a parking meter, yapping, flipping their car keys.

We're walking east when a couple guys come tumbling out of The Burger Barn. This drunken rounder and the Greek cook entangled in each other's arms. They wrestle onto the sidewalk, crashing around, fists flying.

We stop to watch as a crowd quickly gathers. A circle of hard, mongrel faces, gawking greed. Jeering, shouting advice, making bets, making room. Hooting at jokes flung from the back somewhere.

The rounder quickly gets the upper hand, body slamming the Greek into a pile of garbage at the curb. The Greek is giving up about sixty pounds to this saxon giant and screaming for help now, trying to crawl away, the rounder kicking at him wildly.

The waitress/wife is right behind them, shrieking, begging someone to do something. The crowd backs off, keeping her in the circle, making her part of the show. She begins sobbing, her hands limply out in front, grease-sweat hair coming apart. She moves stiffly toward her husband, his face now like bloody hamburger.

"Ah, the mighty Greeks," the Duke nods, looking on.

"What Greeks?" I say. "Last time I looked they were still Christians."

"Boy, you're really getting bitter, Nick."

"You're right, this is terrible. I should go up to the Danforth and do a little folk dancing. Really get into it. Maybe I'll burn down a restaurant."

The cops show up. Climb out of their cruiser, pulling at the crotch of their pants, putting on their hats. They push through the milling crowd, tackle the drunk and cuff him. The Greek is on his knees, clutching his balls, head

15

pitched foward onto the sidewalk. A steady drip of black blood runs from his broken mouth. Disoriented and terrified, he instinctively cowers as his wife approaches like an apparition. She sits next to him, carefully gathers her man into her arms and begins slowly rocking him.

The cops drag the rounder over to the car and throw him into the back seat. They tell everyone to move along, get lost. We linger for a moment, watch the ambulance pulling up for the Greek.

☜

And the night blows. Already yawning, feeling itself all over. Tirades rain down from second storey windows. News of great discoveries made behind the rooming house toilet, roaches that can pick tomorrow's daily double.

Down along at the corner of Bathurst Street we pass the Indian winos lounging on the bank steps. Management trainees of the Canadian Imperial Bank of Canard. Hissing, yelping, blurred figures wrapped in oil soaked rags.

"Hey, guys, how's it going?" the Duke greets them, waving in a generous arc.

They answer with daring feats of acrobatics. Running stagger into a parked car. One foot pirouette and head dive into the pavement. Open hand palm up to bleeding head then look at the hand covered in blood, amazed. Garden of smashed and empty bitters bottles around the steps, piss shadows hanging on the bank's gray stone facade.

"Hey," one of them slobbers, "you got any money?"

The Duke pulls out a few coins, throws them at their feet. Slo-mo scramble, epileptic athletes chasing the loose ball.

"I don't wanna touch them," he shrugs. "Those guys are filthy, man. The lice'll jump right offa them. They're a

16

goddamn breeding ground."

We cross Bathurst against the light, over to the Galaxy
Donuts corner. Its few remaining marquee bulbs flash
erratically, throwing a jagged light into the transit shelter
that serves as a communal vomit bath. Streetcar driver
holds up blaring traffic, yelling at a Portuguese cleaning
woman stuck in the doors.

The freak sisters are hanging around the doorway of the
donut shop, getting ready to go back to work.

"Hi guys, where yu goin?"

Rosie, you're a crippled dwarf. A crippled dwarf with
OHIP crutches. Where do you put them when a john
bites, in the trunk? How about your friend here, this gimp
in the wheelchair. What's she do? Chain it to a telephone
pole?

No, stupid. Her boyfriend watches it.

Oh.

"I dunno," I say to her, "maybe down to the Cameron
for a few. Who knows, it's still early."

"Maybe for you it is. What time is it? Seven, seven-
thirty? These johns been down here since after work. It's
Friday, y'know."

The Duke's feeling expansive this summer night. Must
have had his weekly shower today. He's jocular, telling a
guy in a hopped yellow Corolla to "fix your fuckin
muffler!" Pitching pennies at the born-again turpentine
addict slumped near our feet, he turns to the girls, double
chin, all smiles. "So, ladies, good money tonight?"

"Not bad," says the wheelchair, lighting a smoke. "But
these cops, man, what a pain in the ass. The old guys are
alright. You can blow em and they piss off. It's these
young twirps with the little fag moustaches. Fuck, they
really got it jammed sideways."

"She's right," says Rosie, her eyes moving like radar in
a slow 180. "They're jealous, y'know. On a big night I can

17

make almost as much as those rookie wieners take home in a week. Some of em say I gotta give em a cut. I say, fuck you, take me in then. It's a big hassle to em though and I just gotta stay back from the curb for a while. They know I'll get off in the end. I mean, fuck, look at me."

Yeah, Rosie, look at you. You're the little dreamboat of a billion middle-aged stiffs. All getting weekend hard-ons, keeping the old gas guzzler in the garage just for you.

After a few brew, on the way to see the Blue Jerks or any old time you feel like it, boys. Rosie here'll give you the best condom blow this side of Yonge Street. But, hey, she don't come cheap, fellas. She's our prize, our little Rosie. She's our special custom model.

The third jewel in this triple crown comes waddling out of the donut shop, half a cruller stuck in her face. Joanne and her tent-sized mumu capitalized on her gland problem a long time ago.

My name is Jo Anne. Like two names, y'know? With a capital J and a capital A.

Alright, I'll keep that in mind. Say, how do you pack yourself into those Japanese econoboxes? Tell me that, Jo Anne.

Simple, bonehead. I make the deal on the corner and then walk into the lane behind. He swings his legs out the driver's side door so I can blow him like that. See?

Uh, yeah. I get it.

"You guys got girlfriends? I never see youz with girls." Rosie's worried about us.

"Naw," sniffs the Duke, looking down the street, "can't afford a girlfriend."

"It's expensive," I agree. "You think you can just take them to some diner like The Stem? Or drink at The Paddock over here? You gotta have a couple c-notes just for weekends these days. Besides, what do yu need a girlfriend for? It's not that hard to get laid. Not yet, anyway."

18

Rosie frowns, taking this in.

The Wheelchair knows better though. "They can pay too," she sticks in. "I mean, if they're workin they should put in some money too."

Been reading the papers, Wheelchair?

The Duke gets harsh, skeptical. "You think so, eh? All this women crap. It's like somekinda Nazi propaganda. Anyway, who cares? We're just the boys, y'know? I don't need that pressure. Some barkin dog always whining at me, chewing my ear off... They'll get yu workin all the pulleys at once. Workin like ten coolies. Finger up her ass, twirlin their clit, going like a piston...forget it..." He turns his head and spits, dismissing it all with a sour face.

"He's right," I say, "it's all work."

The three of them look at each other.

Our three graces.

$

A streetcar load of sidewinders goes clattering by down Bathurst Street to the stadium. An important game tonight. All kinds of noisy Scarborough type suburban hicks, already pissed, hollering their guts out. Couple times a week they get let out of those concrete filing cabinets out in the sticks and come down here making this street worse than usual.

The girls all wave. The goofs on the street car go haywire. Jugulars throbbing, pasty faces gone beet red.

"We'll get some on the way back," says fat Jo Anne.

To Rosie it's a given. "For sure. They'll be comin in threes and fours, especially if the Blue Jays win. Yu take em behind the bank one at a time, or their friends watch sometime and there's like a couple hundred in 20 minutes, max."

The Wheelchair's boyfriend comes up doing the Parkdale apeboy strut. He's got his chin high, eyes mean squint, thin lips in almost a whistle.

"Hey, what's happenin?" the Duke smiles, trying to put him at ease.

Apeboy smells us over, relaxes slightly. Takes off his filthy baseball cap, runs a hand through the blonde shag. "Alright," he finally grunts.

Wheelchair's gazing up at him with those cotton candy blue eyes. Childish whitetrash eyes that haven't changed for him since she was fourteen. He looks down at her, leaning on one leg, bunch of keys hanging off his waist. Puts away his pit bull face for her, brings out the low mutter, "...hey, baby..." His hand meets her cheek and her eyes close.

The other two look away, full of respect. They'll talk about it later in warm voices, tell her how lucky she is.

"He's really good to yu, honey. That guy loves yu, baby, and he's so good lookin too."

"I know. Me and Doug been together a long time. His mother died a few years ago, eh, and I moved in with him. He takes care of everythin, he really wants me to be happy."

Rosie and Jo Anne nod like a couple of pentecostals hearing about something moving and miraculous.

4

My old pal.

The one who got into the U of T. The one who's paying unbelievable rent. Time we drove along Bloor Street in the snow, stoned on mescaline with very fresh bodies and terrible hallucinations. Yeah, brother, we could rock like hell then and comparing the size of our dicks was a good bond of trust.

My good old buddy with the renovated attitude. You once dealt like a carpetbagger and every lifestyle mag in the city has covered your recovery. It was funny running into you on the street. The Duke cringing at the introduction, mumbling: "Who's the suit?"

The suit and me, we jerked off behind his parents garage, we sniffed glue and did all that cheap acid. The suit and me planned on how we'd murder our families and then escape on a Maple Leaf Lines bus headed for the sun. We were dead sure it was the only way to get a hold of what we wanted more than anything. To be named Richard Stephenson and Stephen Richardson instead of Nikolaos Hondrokephalopoulos and Haralambos Kolovalvidas.

But, my old pal, you seem to have figured the percentages and made the adjustment. Nice haircut.

Looking real white now, the unhyphenated Canadian. Sure, let's have a drink sometime. When you've got a second I'll be down at the local, you know the place. I'll be trading debts with those sardonic bitches who are so tired of shaving their legs they're thinking of having them amputated. I set you up with them good. You haven't lost it. No, man, don't worry. Some lace, black, boots. Finalists from the Professional Hairbag Championships. White chalk skin and bad beer kidneys, nic-stained fingers. I'll make sure they got their shots. You know I would do anything for you. Nothing can come between us. Not even the idea that there's more to living than just a future. I will always be here. No shoes on my hooves, with scarred pelt and split shins, marrow running out my bones. I will wait and you will see me. Lean, a hung man.

▮

The Duke's watching my long lost bud drive away. "Who's *that* guy?" he asks, disgusted. It bugs him. The car, the clothes, but mostly because the guy was in a hurry and had no interest.

"An old friend of mine," I say. "Knew him when we were kids."

"What a weirdo..."

"I dunno. He's just some office geek now. You know what happens..."

"He's dead," the Duke grimaces. "See him? His head's like a pork roast with a couple raisins stuck in it. Must be a cop... It's depressing. Mortgaged off his nuts for a wallpapered dog cage down in that concrete curtain at the harbourfront. His wife gettin stuffed by the pool cleaner five minutes after she sends him and the kids out the door. I wouldn't bust my ass for some retread so she can be givin head to the plumber... Nick, you know some real suckers..."

Forget it, you could rip out your own eyes trying to ignore this dazzled midday. Stop and stare at these chatty luncheon line-ups for the more popular eateries. Mouths of the possessed open at me, gossiping manhole covers. Cut into one of these Nuremberg style, chrome-plated booteeks, finger the upscale merchandise. Yards of leather shoulder pads and high impact Kruppware. Try chatting up the shop-assistant.

"Hey, you're alright...what's your name?"

"Where do you guys hang out?"

"You know," says the Duke, leaning heavy into the triangular counter, casual as hell. Gives her a thin, jaded voice. "We hang out here and there. We're the old boys... We don't need this hype, just come and go. Lookin into this an that..."

She's got a pit in her stomach, needs filling. Contact lense aqua eyes flutter, creamy tits heave up under the black leather bodice.

"I've seen you guys before," she says cooly.

"Oh yeah?" I smile at her, "yeah, we're neighbourhood guys. Not like these nine-to-fivers. You do anything else besides this?"

"I'm an artist," she replies in a low voice.

"It's tough. I'm an artist too and you never get a break. I mean, here yu are havin to work in this dump. Getting pimped by a shop owning designer peasant."

"I know," she frowns. "I'm really sick of it. I wanna get a show but these galleries around here are real cliques. Totally stuck up. You gotta know somebody."

"It's like that in this town," sizes the Duke. "Where you from?"

She glances down into the glass counter, her hands straighten out some cards. "Guelph," she answers after a

23

moment, "but I came here a year and a half ago. You guys from here?"

"Sure," I groan, "born here."

"I go to OCA," she tells us, "you know, the art school?"

"Yeah?"

She nods the black mane tease-job, blue nails playing with her silver bracelets. "It's okay but they just use yu, eh. The instructors, they're artists too and they just use the students to do the work so they can get their grants."

Me and the Duke really feel for this girl. He stands, gets serious. "Figures. Sleazy assholes. You don't need that. You got the looks. You could be making two hundred a night in some cocktail place. No, I don't wait in any line-ups. I believe in a free market economy."

Even I can't stand a lot of this after awhile and start going for the door.

The Duke's all with it now, right on top of the deal. He's tall and lean and good looking for a moment. A real charmer, loose and lanky in black peg-legs, nose-pickers and polo shirt. His teasing eyes roam over the shop girl, latching onto something.

"Hey, Nick," he calls after me, "you going? I'll catch you later. I'm gonna stick around for a minute."

The hick behind the counter is gettin into it. We're at least as stupid as her. Tomorrow morning the Duke will file a report over breakfast at Rooneem's.

"Fuck, man, I went out at dawn to get us coffees and when I get back she's standing in the middle of the room drinking rye outa one of those auto-club plastic cups. You know, those spill proof things you suck on. She was just standing there naked with this fat ass. Without the make-up her mug looks like a sideswiped fender. That's it, I've had it. I'm going clean."

24

5

I'm over at Shank's place. He's on the phone, screaming. "Yeah?! You'd better get over here, *now!* I'm gonna fuck you, man!"

My hero. The ultimate driver, malignant success story. Shank is a full blown example of a white-hot economy. Supplier of high-octane fuel and wild ambition. A middle-aged middle weight who was born to boss. But right now he's not too happy. Cheri, his most private friend, has gone quiet the way she does when he's howling. Curled up behind her magazine, she's ignoring the humourless side of the diamond life.

Shank slams the phone down, fuming. Stands over me, across the coffee table, head shoved forward.

"You been with Chops?" he demands.

"No."

"Don't fuck me!" he shouts, a thumb jammed into his own chest. Cheri recedes further into the couch corner.

"Forget about Chops," I say, trying to calm Shank down. "He'll come through."

"Is that right? Then how come he just told me he's flat?"

"What's it for?"

"The quarter ounce. You know that! Quit fuckin around, Nick!"

"Okay, okay...shut up already. What's the big deal? I'll go see him."

"NO!" he bellows, his face exploding at me. "*I* wanna see him!"

Shank's gone right off the deep end now, getting his Protestant rage up. A man of sacred vows and iron principles. Pacing, hands grappling with a cigarette pack, lighting up.

"You know it's not the money, Nick. I did that bastard a personal favour. Fronted him a good little start up. And now this!" He stops, gives me a slack look. "What the fuck's he think he's doing?!"

I'm gazing around at the art prints and knick-knacks in this love nest. "I dunno..."

Shank takes it to heart. Arteries bursting at even the thought of it. Cheri approaches him, the silky golden daughter. Shank's lips distend, his fat hand rests on her shoulder. "It's not you, baby. I'm pissed off at that little prick, Chops. I give the guy a break and he fucks around like this."

She takes his right arm in both her hands, sugar-kiss lips stare up at him. His eyes go down to hers, purple bags hanging over a quivering mouth.

"Go make us some coffee, will yu, hon?"

Pat on the ass sends her off. His eyes follow her, blank. Maybe seeing her ass again the way he saw it the very first time. When he met her about a month ago, Shank made me listen to a couple hours of revelations.

"Got a clean cunt in her," he'd told me. "And she's not stupid, neither. She's got a head."

"Yeah, Shank, I can see it."

"No, I'm serious, man. She's really somethin."

"Yeah? what?"

"I'll take care of her."

✖

"What's with you?" Shank asks, snapping me back. "No time to be sleepin, Nick." He starts pacing again, drumming the cigarette pack on his nails, points at me. "You're still in for two big ones, y'know."

"Yeah, okay..." I answer, wincing, "it's okay..." Now I'm in Chops' league.

"Waddaya mean it's okay? What's okay, Nick?"

"Two G's," I grunt, resting my boots on the coffee table. "Don't be so cheap."

Shank's still shaking his head at me, thick bottom lip stuck out. "You don't look so good," he mumbles. "Maybe you oughta cool out for a while." He turns away, heavy stare out the living room window onto the quiet street. Only a rice burner revving somewhere.

Comes back with a proposition. "Tell you what," he says quickly. "You go get the bread off Chops and I'll do you a taste."

My head rolls back. "Aw...Shank..."

"C'mon," he presses, "it's a square deal. Anyway, he's your buddy, Nick. Just get him over here with the money or bounce him for it. I don't care."

6

"You seen Chops around?"

Stein's stooped on his rotten back steps, mulling over my question. Angles his head upward, one eye shut to the sun. "That guy's a gimp," he finally answers. "Why you lookin for him?"

"I wanna score."

"Off Chops?"

My eyes close for a moment. Stein's forlorn image burned onto the insides of my eyelids. I let out a long breath, feel the heat prickling up my back.

"Help me find him. I gotta get the bread he owes Shank."

Stein's in this frowning sweat, drawn, miserable mouth. "Naw," he grumbles, "I'm not runnin around after that fruit."

"Why not? You're not doing anythin."

"Fuck that," he leans back, putting on a pair of sunglasses. "Why don't you take care of it yourself?"

"I feel bad, man. I'm broke. I don't wanna be doing this. C'mon, don't be an asshole. We'll figure it out."

Stein take a long look down the driveway, guessing at the temperature. "Alright," he gives in, getting to his feet. "He's gone to the Black Bull. He was here a while ago."

☼

We catch Chops sitting alone, ogling at the waitress, his back to the door. Stein comes up behind quickly. "What's cookin, Chops?"

"Shank wants his money," I say flat, sitting down.

"Yeah?" he snorts. "You two workin for him now?"

Stein's smoking in Chops' face, elbows on the table. "C'mon, Chopski, let's get this over with."

Chops is hunched forward, hiding inside the oversized suit jacket. Nervous knee going, hands shredding a match pack. "Christ!" he blurts at us. "I partied you guys for free and now you're screwin me like this. Fuck Shank! Fuck you, too! It's my problem, right?!"

"You little shit," I hiss at him. "What the fuck *are* you doing? Gimme the money."

The tube-top waitress stops to collect the empty glass. Chops looks up at her, turns to me. "I don't have it on me, okay?"

"Where is it?"

"Stashed it over at this chick's place."

"Gimme a break."

Stein glances at me, looks back to Chops. "Let's go get it," he says.

Chops' head is down toward the table, eyes flashing side to side. "Yeah...sure," he answers slowly. "I got it hid out there."

◆

We're walking west along Richmond, past the lumber yard at Portland Street. Hot smell of sawdust, afternoon voices. The minimum wagers eating their lunch on top of scrap piles. The three of us squint up at them as we drift by.

Keep going, past the empty lot on the north-west corner.

A big blue and white sign put up announcing it's soon to be the site of another 40 storey pile of luxury chicken coops. Below the sign winos ride in no wheel cars, simmering in their own stink, nodding in sleep at us. The procession of Chops makes them pull up a hand, wave off a fly. Old men, old dogs, propped up against the rust fender of a blind '64 Fairlane. Lounging under a single withered tree. Scavenging rusty cans and licking sardine lids. Dragging along a mangled shopping cart.

Out of the buzzing quiet a straight-arm shoots up from Stein, catching Chops between the shoulder blades. It sends him staggering forward in a half turn, breathless yelp. Takes my boot in the gut, I miss his nuts. Chops stumbles sideways toward the road, mouth open to yell, swinging at air. Stein's diving at him, both hands on his collar, throwing him to the pavement. That stupid jacket is tearing, coming up over Chops' head. He falls awkward, sound of feet scuffling. I put a boot into his face.

Stein's glancing around, panting, squats next to Chops. "Drag him over to the lot," he whispers, "let's get him off the road."

Chops is lying here at my feet. His head in his hands, crying and cursing us. Knees pulled up to his chest. Blood spitting out of him, shining wild red on the bleached sidewalk.

"Nick!" Stein craws at me. "Wake up! You want the cops around or what?"

We get Chops behind the abandoned building on the other side of the lot, the boarded up pile of bricks in the middle of that short block between Queen and Richmond. Each of us with an arm, Chops dragging his feet maybe more than a man in his condition really has to.

Dump him onto a piss-cured mattress between overflowing trash cans. Me and and Stein collapse on either side. Chops is crying in muffled bursts, hands smeared with his own wounds. The front of his dirty

30

white shirt's splattered with blood, blackred oozing down from his mouth. Christ, you'd think we cut the bastard's throat.

I leave them and go get coffees from the Woolworth's nearby and napkins for Chops. Coming back I see Stein bent over, one arm loose around Chops' shoulders, talking real close, as if he's kissing him. A guy trying to make up with an upset girlfriend.

A few of the skids have rolled over in our direction, showing a small interest. Layed out in the shade, drowsy eyed, slowly fanning themselves with pieces of ripped cardboard.

Chops is whimpering and snivelling, wadding blood into the bunched up tissue. He's calling us cocksuckers and cheap-shots and faggots and everything else.

Stein's relaxed, patient, wearing the gag store sunglasses, sitting there concentrating on his shoes. He examines them this way an that. Spits onto his fingers and rubs it into the worse scuff marks.

I'm sinking coma-hot dizzy, nerve beginning to chafe. Stein give me a slight nod. Chops' hand shakes its way into his pocket, pulls out a fold of c-notes and tosses them between my legs.

"I was gonna pay him..." he shivers, fingers going back to his bloody mouth.

I grab the money. Stein's up on his feet, jacking up his pants, brushing off his ass, on the move and turns to me.

"So? What are yu doin? Let's go."

I watch Chops pull himself up against the wall of the building. He gathers his knees into his arms.

"Fuck him! C'mon, Nick!"

-W-

31

We begin our recoil up through those narrow, chicken-shed streets north of Queen, west of Bathurst. Past immigrant lawn altars sporting hand-painted statues of the virgin. Giving thanks for the aluminum sided, small windowed dive housing three generations of thick-headed serfs.

A beady-eyed, barrel-shaped matrone is out watering her postage stamp piece of turf. She watches suspiciously as me and Stein go by. Defensively clams around her own thoughts of her bearded daughters.

Trudging through this deaf jail sweat. Up the corridors of a deaf and dumb afternoon. No men around during the day. All lined up at the UI office or drywalling a donut shop in Woodbridge.

For a few seconds at a time I walk with my eyes closed. Thinking only to keep walking, just get there, through this death zone full of Pope lovers and Workmen's Comp frauds.

Stein turns to me with a sharp voice. "You think Shank'll let us nod there?"

"I dunno, I guess so."

Words melt down in this light. The trick is to just keep walking past these miserable old bastards sitting on their front porches, guarding the rathole fire trap they slaved for for thirty years. Still haven't learned any English, eh, shit-for-brains?

Stein's scanning the ground, checking every inch of pavement. Doubles over quick here and there. Loose piece of tin-foil, a dime, pack of matches, losing lottery ticket. Slaps at garbage piled up neat in front of houses. He points out cars.

"That's not bad with a five speed, the automatic's a pig. A pick-up truck, that's a good one, the Mazda. Cheaper than most, good motor... Yeah, I'm gonna get a little job somewhere and live alone. No more of this bullshit, I wanna buy a car..."

32

7

†

Shank's on the back deck with Cheri in her bikini. Her body's tan hidden tits and dyed blonde pubes under the white stretch. She sits up sudden, her body crying out for us, wanting to take us in with a cold cloth on the forehead. Her eyes cut over to Shank, her lips part, sees him, she lies back and says nothing.

"Fuck," Shank laughs, "did you guys run up here?"

The sun is his friend. It dances up and down the glass of iced tea or cold piss he's drinking. It rolls across his mirrored shades, glistens off his oiled flab. His new set of caps grin up at us. I toss the money on the white plastic table next to him. Shank's sprawled out on the padded lawn chair half turned toward us, half smiling. He gets up without a word, counting the money, goes somewhere into his vault.

Cheri twists around from her tanning mat, this strained look from behind her sunglasses. "You guys okay?"

In a few minutes Shank returns and hands me a tiny envelope cut from the center spread of a porn mag.

"That wasn't too bad, eh?" he says, patting me on the back.

"No," I answer. "Made things clear all around."

"It's just over a point," he goes on, getting back into his chair. "But not here, eh, guys?"

Stein's still all business. "Well, at least give us a clean fit then."

Shank's washed his hands and doesn't want to get up again. He groans, arms dropping to his sides. Struggles to his feet and signals us to follow. Takes a wrapped 100U out of a kitchen cupboard and herds us toward the door.

"Sorry, guys, I'm expecting some people. You don't mind, eh?"

✳

On the sidewalk again. Little spic kids stop their racket, stare up at us. Stein reaches out, pats one of them on the head, hearts of mothers around the world seize up.

Hey, kid, feelin bored?

And he's agitated, raking his hair real hard. "Where we gonna cook this? I thought that fuck would at least give us a minute."

"Let's go to my place," I say.

Stein's not too excited by that. Bug-eyed, looks up and down the street. "Aw...man," he whines, "all the way back down to Queen?...I know, let's go to Arlene's. She'll be at work, we can get in through the fire escape."

Arlene's this thin, cool ghost who's gladly paying three quarters of what she earns to live in a two room hallway at College and Grace. Holds the rent down by letting the gum-rotted, semi-deaf Macedonian landlord shuffle his hand in his pocket whenever he talks to her. Small time scene-queen who finally fulfilled her life's ambition and got a job in a hep second-hand clothing store in Kensington market. Now she can leopard her hair any colour she likes, bolt on the bondage gear anyway she wants.

Her little kitchen is dim, faucet dripping into a sink full of dirty pans. Cat complains about our bad karma. On the fridge door there's a collection of kitsch postcards, scraps, a poster of a guitar player caught in mid-yowl.

Clock quietly ticking and I wander through Arlene's small life in two rooms. Magazine shots torn out and miserably framed over the single bed. Last year's heels pitched into the corner, spilling out of a closet full of vintage rags, all of them black. Melted down purple candles stuck to the top of the dresser amid used containers of make-up and long forgotten cassettes. Cigar box crammed with broken old lady jewellery. Nothing worth stealing. The good life.

Her whole apartment hung with a stale gas stove stink and I'm leaning in the kitchen door watching Stein bend a spoon.

"Christ," he's griping, still in a knot about what it takes, "the things you gotta do just to get off these days."

He sits at the rickety kitchen table, surrounded by the endless collection of odds and ends, coated in grease, growing together as Arlene grows older. Stein's hands go quickly, economy of movement. He's hunting for the vein, slapping his arm. Fuck the tie, this vein will rise on it's own. He wants to go first. First user's always safer. Or is it he's so in love he can't wait?

I've already got my vein picked out. Big, blue, aching. I'm pumping my fist, getting butterflies, grinning involuntarily.

Stein's fast, manic but clinical, making the most of his good luck. Easing out the spike, holding it upward. He sets it down carefully, a jelly milk drip slides out the end, falls back into the mix. Who knows what's in *his* blood.

I'm fumbling, clammy nerves knocking against this goddamn soup spoon. Get that bubble out. Middle of the vein, break the worm.

➤

35

Dusk coming in through Arlene's kitchen window. That soft gray colour running down alley-ways. Sounds of the world getting home from work. We're muttering, calm, whites of the eyes tinted blue.

Door slams downstairs. Arlene's click-clack up the steps. Stein gives me a weak, pained face.

"What the fuck?!" she finds us, her eyes nailing the job to the table. "I'm gonna call the cops! Get outa here! Get outa my house!"

We're up and shifting, hands wiping off on pant legs. Trying to talk out of bone dry mouths, tongues covered in sand. Arlene's face pulled out of shape, yelling, lips racing. Cheap mascara bleeding around her eyes. Those little tits rising, dropping.

Stein's got his hands up like a conductor. "Sorry, we were just..."

"Fuck you, man! Get out!"

We're moving toward the stairs, tripping over each other. Her chewed down fingers twisting, she's pushing at me, mouth ripped down cold, shrill tears. Anger from all day and anger from all night. Arlene, I want to ask you to dance. Let me take you in my arms and explain while I show you these steps.

*

Crawl sideways back down south. It's cooler now, more cars parked in the streets. Easier to slide between the sheets with dark, dried blood islands floating there. Whose is whose?

My landlady's there when I get back. No, c'mon, have some mercy, but she's talking away. Quit your babbling. Neurotic, mid-thirties mutt. Do I need to hear about the Green Party coming around and how I gotta go vote at some ex-hippie's house up the road? Hey, lady, I don't talk to nobody who's wearing socks and sandals, get me?

Yeah, yeah...you know all the names. You've got the right friends who have friends and okay, there was a big romance for you in there somewhere years ago. You were maybe a pretty good piece then but this is now and face it, you got this half-renovated termite shack and you got me renting a room and the upstairs kitchen. You see the welfare cheque coming through the slot and it makes you feel; "Well, he'll be paying again. At least he's got that figured out."

I may seem totally raked out but I see how you been so depressed ever since your young thing took off without a word. Those sweet, eighteen year-old muscles you'd run your fingers along, admiring his chest when he'd be on top, proud you could own such a powerful pony. Betrayed in the end by your own shifty-eyed judgement and tight fist. But you'll survive. Business is good, you've got a hairless body and the rent is safe.

You hate introducing me to those career friends of yours as much as you hate them meeting your east-end, hick brother. It's alright, I'll stay out of the way as usual. You'll only hear my steps squeaking up above while you're all drinking herbal tea and talking about people you know who aren't there.

I'll be up in the attic. Once again staring at the picture I hang on to. Black and white snapshot, unfocused, bent and curling toward me. Searching that square of fragments, finding a peculiar little man. Is that a man? What is this thing with a big head and sticks for arms? Evasive, allowing only half an image. Dodging in front of a simple wooden house sliced off at the frame edge. A taken mouth. Acquired secretly, the rare and priceless motive stolen from his inflamed temper and hoard of custom porn.

But that poor guy, he is absolved by naive urges he never understood. Overwhelmed, utterly defeated in his war to eliminate the collective memory. A man with four limbs, stretched out, his mouth, his strong teeth grasping. Who once entered this country young, virile and eager to assimilate, to become the soul of post-war success, a New Canadian.

His was among the mob of bright and anxious faces arriving by steamship at Halifax during the spring of 1956. Taken by CN Rail to Toronto, destined to pave its muddy streets. Unloaded at Union Station, a slow stepping tumble of amber cloud, mute foreign voices. The soft noise of tired feet moving up Yonge Street, to begin a new life, nine to a room. Always looking up first, making sure the sky was the same here.

He and his olive skinned wife came as part of a huge, snaking beast, headless but strong. Willing to work, to put their backs into this place. Meandering line of dark-eyed immigrants, frightened by the mythical size of Canada. Furtive, homesick and suspicious. Dragging bundles and sick parents, crying children and pregnant bellies. Carrying cardboard suitcases and tireless grudges from the old country. Appreciating their great good fortune and promising to cause no trouble.

Though back then, that clever little guy, he was convinced that in this country he and his offspring would finally escape the tribal blood feuds and balkan vendettas. Delivered unto the bosom of Canada, finally freed from the rotten yoke of obsolete responsibilities, reborn in the miracle of wide open space.

But it cut him down when his young wife remained close to those unwritten rituals, passed down only by gesture and glance. At dusk he would find her watching the eastern sky, suffocating their cramped little flat with frankincense, filling it with those goddamn icons.

It turned his blood to piss to see her embroidering patiently for hours. Each meticulously stitched pillow case and table cloth clawing him back to the village, to its unbending language. He would be overcome with a crying rage to find his mother, his wife's mother, those two old crones they'd brought with them, spending the whole evening sitting in the dark to save on Hydro, gazing out the window, silent as caves. He was emasculated by their grinding disappointment and relentless scheming, left to feel speechless and lonely that these women could make this land seem so empty when he knew it to be full. Cursing them, he vowed to himself to Anglicize his name and put many highway miles on the car he was determined to buy.

In earnest he had tried to explain to his wife what tormented him but she could only reassure him with a few words in a dialect he did not want to hear. And when he looked through his tears into her marble black eyes he knew his bride would forever remain a fearful peasant with a grave mistrust of the new world.

Her hands became red and swollen from endless hours on the line at Philips. Savings were saved but her tongue would not turn and slowly she began to stiffen. Her husband felt the aching coldness of their bed and he began to pray. He prayed to his god and beat her as he prayed. He sat her down and fell to his knees, beseeching her and promising anything.

Eventually, a real Canadian doctor had to be called in. Those pills you gave her, Mr. Doctor, they were good for a lot of things. She got stoned and lost her doubt, working happily, her tongue loosened by the joy of department store catalogues.

It seemed appealing so I began skimming those little yellow beauties. An undetected parasite on her habit, stoned on a drug designed to calm crazy immigrant women. A drifting, all-seeing, headless little first-generation man. It became clear I was born in *this* country.

▼

"Phone..." Landlady calls up the stairs. "Do you want me to tell them to call back?"

I pick it up without answering her.

"Nick, baby," the Duke is there, "what's the deal? I ran into Stein, he told me about Chops."

"We fixed him," I say, grinding my voice. "Taught him a thing or two about manners... So, what you up to?"

"I dunno... You guys got off today, eh?"

"Well, it worked... Hey, how's it going with the Guelph number?"

"Oh, boy!" he roars. "She's a load of trouble! I'm backin up the tow motors, the fork lifts, throwin in the anvils. I'm thinkin I just can't fill her up!" The sweet conspiracy.

"Come down," says the Duke. "I got some good hash. Not that Kensington putty. We'll smoke, cool out. You sound baffed."

"No kiddin. We had this thing with Arlene today. It was hard enough gettin a cheap little nod together, then she balls it up."

"Yeah, Stein told me. Rough day. See yu in a while."

"Okay," and I hang up. Duke, that was good of you. I want you to know I love you for that. The Duke comes out into the stormy weather in a yellow rain slicker, rowing furiously over the giant waves. A pipe between his teeth, strong arms and legs, throwing his weight into the oars. Out into the wine dark sea.

8

We're new men sitting around the Duke's warehouse hideout. A friendly group shot. Almost nightfall. Tin transistor buzzing in the corner. Sun sets its colours out the window along the Gardiner Expressway. Squeal and clang of trains in the yard down there.

Gathered around the salvaged kitchen table, hash joints going and a mickey of LCBO scotch. Even Chops shows up. He's been to Western General. A couple blackblood stitches in the middle of his swelled and purple bottom lip. Chops is pissed off with me and Stein at first, won't sit down or have a drink. Just stands by the door, brooding.

We're surrounded by the garbage picked miracles the Duke has so mercifully saved. Tonight, as host, he keeps the fires burning.

"Listen," he says, "these things happen, right? It was a drag but yu all shoulda known better."

Stein has no problem with this and Chops wants so bad to be back in the fold. Anyway, where would you go, Chops? We're gonna buy you the brand new bike in the store window, keep the promise to take you to the midway at the Ex. We'll go out tonight, together, closer than sisters without a father.

" "

Later on in the Cameron Pub. Sitting along the wall sucking on draft, in our private group. Broken-backed shtick art hanging behind us. Brow beaten children of the politically correct.

Handsome Ned is doing his western solo croon in the back room, and that's call for a real dress up. All the pointed shoes and raggedy hemmed debutantes are up for it. I can hear Ned winding them up for 'Ghost Riders In the Sky' and Elvis is rumbling out of the juke box. The Blue Jays are losing on tv.

Cassandra comes swishing by in her pancake, savage black hair, barbarian leather gear and thirty pounds of jangling hardware. Giving us the nose but she'll be back. It's another snob-off since those days me and her would hole up in her broom closet of a room at the Black Bull Hotel. Those cold-snap nights she'd be moaning about potency freaks. Newspaper cut-outs of super-stud cunt crushers like MuMu Gaddafi pinned up on her walls. Her voice so salty, writhing that ass on the bed.

"He's a real man..."

In the street-lit dark, your head hanging off the edge when I'm trying to push through you and the make-up only made you look older. Seeing you go mute, slush blood full of tired demons. The night is out there, Cassandra, just outside this window. I remember freezing below your room, bouncing pennies off the glass. Half naked you came down those crooked stairs, playing the hurt kitten. Swashbuckling staggering drunk, I carried you back up the steps to your burrow. The icy leather I'm in getting your nipples so hard like my prick, pissed on beer, calling your name because it knows you will always be there. Old men in the rooms around us, infirm nazis maybe. Leaving their doors open to hear you better, watery cum mixing with their weak bladders. You despised me for wanting to scrape the mud off your face

42

and burn those cheap rags. Trying to force you through my early dreams, clean you out and teach you to be a good wife. You've got your own condoms, expensive ones which never break, not letting any cock poison your eggs.

You remember when we stumbled into this bar drunk that time? There was my main uptown squeeze all done up just for me. Coming back to claim me with her precious pawn ticket.

Yeah, Cassandra, it's true. I dropped you like a boring party and I was embarrassed to be with you. Seeing her in rich black velvet, her hat worth more than you and me put together. She's the one who could get me to shave and put on a clean shirt. Tell me to cut my nails and wash out my cock before showing up with a bottle that had to be from France. She had books lining her bedroom walls, insulating those polite shrieks. My nigger cock was into white flesh, you see. It is so, Cassandra.

○

Cassandra sits with us in the Cameron tonight. Stein's a grinning jackal, expecting some fireworks. But she don't give a fuck now. This week it's some drummer or bass player or VJ.

Me and the Duke got our faces close in a huddle under cover of all this noise. A couple art hags across the room check us out, keeping the ice on while looking away. They got these hard, skinny bodies. Real tight in black and a whole sack of unreasonable demands, I'm sure. The Duke covets them like I do, knowing their disgust.

"Those two are alright," he says, draining another glass. "But, c'mon, you need that? Man, you gotta be somekinda turbocharged fag to get into them. You know how it is. Be sensitive, be discreet but tough. Keep your mouth shut most of the time and they think you know what's happenin."

43

"It's true," I shrug. "All this talk."

"Oh yeah," the Duke agrees. "You gotta screw their heads first."

"Anyway," I say, "they're not exactly in love with us."

No, probably not. Guys like us, we wouldn't even wash our hands before touching them. Yeah, we'd take our socks off to fuck with them but wouldn't put the toilet seat down after taking a piss and we'd always read the back of old love postcards without asking.

I'd want nothing else but to be close to you though chances are good I'll turn out like your father and you'd get sick of that pretty fast. I'd wanna get you pregnant, then forget about it. You'd have to pay the rent and I'd try to make up for it by thinking that when I take you in my arms and you catch my skunk sweat it'll make everything alright. My breath full of sour bad teeth and you know the smell coming out of me is some other cunt. Could even be one of your friends.

Your eyes are sharp now, a wolverine with clear skin. You're in the bar, holding up every mug shot next to a list of quality control standards. Checked me twice and then crossed off. How do I get under the floodgates? Dig my fingers in on either side of your spine and get a grip of those venus ribs. Pull it open, make you watch the clock and think about intimate gifts I might like. How proud will you be when I'm leaving deep bruises on the inside of your thigh? How much more will you love me when I take a polaroid of your cunt and carry it around in my wallet?

9

⚓

Out boozing with Lacey, the classic Yank. Six-foot four, rock-jawed John Wayne fan with an easily offended attitude. Don't mention Vietnam. He's another American emigré success story in this land of the sort of free. One of Shank's free trade partners.

It's only a Chicago asshole like Lace who can grab an Avenue Road uptown husband by the lapels and tell him all about etiquette. It's strictly routine, the wives look us over as if we're the bank balance. Getting the edge they read about in fashion glossies reeking of perfume samples.

On Queen West again, at the bar in the Peter Pad Resto. Leaning forward, trying to get a good look at a computer jock's date. Fancy piece with her expensive underwear on, I can tell. All kind of sheer and rosebud clasps and who knows what else, sweet scented closets and heart shaped soaps in the can.

But Lace is bored by this crap. He don't drink much and never touches flesh so he's up marching past the crowded booths, kicking at legs sticking out.

"Mind your foot, sir, please, the staff, thanks a lot... Anything else you'd like?"

Up and down, big stride, asking for ID, gestapo officer on a train load of collaborators. Comes back to the bar with an armload of red wine cunt prints on the bar's logo napkins. Inspects them careful, right up to his face.

"Seen that one before," I say, pointing.

Lacey smirks like I'm soft in the head. "You're really messed up, man," and he pulls his warhead prick out of the vintage Denver Prior suit, skewering the print. "This is me gettin sexually assaulted," he cracks. "If you had half a brain you'd be carryin a polaroid."

Our floor show gets the Liberace waiters in a bad flex, stealing their rectal thunder. The office tower chick is heating up, though she knows it's just not possible to pay to see this kinda act. Sorry, honey, back to whale sperm and swamp mud for you.

Lacey's cop head searches around, making decisions. "Let's get outa here," he orders. "This place is worse than the terminal ward at a veterinary hospital."

He leads me out the door and across the road to the Rivoli, the gray plywood dump with the smarmy bartender. A secretary who looks like a drag queen gets me stoned in the can.

"I love your hair," she purrs. "Is it really that dark?"

"Sure, I'm a natural guy."

Hanging off the bar, drinking fart-flavoured schnapps. Lacey patrols the four foot semi-circle in front of me, pulling on his chin, constantly patting down the patent leather hair. Every couple minutes he drags over another black-haired, blood-lipped weekend wonder and shoves her face to mine.

"Hey, wake up!" he yells. "You want this one?"

Open my eyes to a faded I-D cover. A picture painted onto the dry surface of one more clerk from North York.

"What's the matter?" he keeps shouting. "Doncha just wanna *have* her?!"

If I had a million I'd hire a Wop to ruin his suit.

Lacey's suddenly holding this cold pose, pulls up his frame Bugsy Siegel style. "Hey, look, mister," his hands

46

wide, open at me. "I just wanna meet a sweet girl and give her my love."

"Yeah? You gonna wash your cock before or after you fuck her?"

Lacey's big, clean hands swing together over his balls, finding and holding each other. Feet apart, the Vegas doorman. His head rolls back, so disappointed, and he gives me the facts.

"If I didn't consider you a close personal friend, which is not a light thing for me, man, I'd be writing yur headstone. This is aside from the fact you're an Aries with Cap rising and are born on the same day as this girl who used to do my pedicure until I booted her teeth down her throat for commenting, in what I felt to be a less than professional manner, about the hair on my toes."

I'm warned.

"So remember," he keeps up, "get along with me." Turning to leave he stops, looks back. "Oh, if you wanna call me, wash out your mouth first, huh?" And his wide-leg, cock-free strut stomps out into a dead Queen Street night.

So Lacey leaves me here with the hi-tech ditch diggers. These bad bodies strapped into boutique nightmares, eating salads with cute names. Immigrants from boring teen times in Winnipeg. Alberta hicks come to make it big in my good ol' home town. Thank god it's almost closing time.

Rush up the street to make last call at the Cameron. Packed on weekends with the jerk-offs stupid enough to line up and I gotta sneak in the side door. Get into the back room, see which initialized band is giving over. Work my way through a yelling mob crowd, make for the juke box in the front barn.

"Hey, where you been?!"

"Just got here! What speaks are on?!"

Kevin's in my boat. All the war paint's on around us. Packed noise, hair sticking up, some racket left in the world.

"Liberty Street!" he hollers at me, "Split a cab?!"

"Yeah..."

I'm looking through the jammed bodies for some familiar gash. Maybe one of those undergrads I introduced to this bar. On a blunt hook for a few weeks if I can bother to answer the phone. They come down on their own sometimes asking for me. With beer money, dope if they can somehow manage to score. Somebody's over-aged daughter finally hitting the hustings, disappointed to see what's under the leather and boot braces. But your body's not much better than mine, sinking twenty-two year old tits. Why don't you get some fucking exercise?

Kevin's lips at my ear, rasp yell. "Let's do some lines in the can!"

Pushing through the crowd. Carrot-top says hi. I grab her ass, her rude smile.

"Liberty tonight," I tell her.

She nods, loses all immediate interest in me. She's standing over this neo-retro rocker with tattoos down both his arms. He's pointing, talking: "...and then the little squirrel said to his friend the fox..."

Squeeze sideways into the toilet. *ST. GEORGE LIVES* in red paint above the urinals. So does the dragon, buddy.

♣

About four o'clock at the speak on Liberty, down behind Lamport Stadium, near the lakefront. Jake's filled the place, that always seems to make him nervous. Tony Kenney's pick-up rockabilly crew is kickin out. Patches of piss and puke on the sides of the building, baby-making sessions in the scrap-wrecks at the autobody next door.

I see something leaning near the can.

Hey can't you piss outside? You gotta look at your dick or somethin? The can's only for girls.

For girls. She's playing with her beer bottle, slowly peeling the label, wagging her head to the music, crowd hopping in front of her.

Blonde peroxide true haired black spike job dead white deadpan blood mouth false nails eyes bluer than true blue lashes like spiders legs. And she was much more beautiful than even that. Rough initials cut into her marble with a cheap variety store pen knife. Carved oblong hearts:

LOU G. WAS HERE

I'm up against her, checking for a pulse.

"You in a band?" she asks, giving me a little credit. "I think I've seen you before."

Yeah, yeah, I'm in a band. You want my cock stuck into you? C'mon, why not? Tomorrow's Sunday, nobody works.

Hands locked, sutured in the back of a cab heading east on King Street. To your small room in a shared house. Cats winding in out our legs, arms. Your tiny iron mouth giving the text book perfect blow job. My face pushed right into your corroded cunt, salt stain withered. No kid would wanna live in there. Kisses full of overloaded bedside ashtrays. Stale water shared in the middle of the night from a green plastic glass. We become entangled, suicidal hydra. Grip of thighs, ass, cellulose, gasping stranger. Thick stink comes up from under the sheets. Gray web of floating moutains, rolling, restless, smell of another body from another time saved in the old pillow. Your cunt on my breath, lipstick smear on my prick. The last stand late rising holdouts of the Unemployment Insurance Commission.

Drizzling late morning shower with the room-mate's crappy shampoo. Radio from down the hall blabbers opinion poll results. Honey, 51% love our style.

Gaze down between our bodies in the wet, in the feeble

light. Gray white white gray, nearly transparent. Your nipples purple, my hands wax. Open your mouth, no tongue in there. Mute pierces my guts. Her lips splintered, running body caught in the headlights. Suffering animal calls from the distant night time cornfield. Ideas of revenge, an eye for every dread moment.

She takes away the coffee cups and kicks me out so she can sit at her mirror and carefully apply each mangled expectation, her drug store martyr mask that is the source of fashion industry fortunes.

10

I'm up at Shank's place with the Duke, trying to weasel a discount score. The Duke's on the couch next to me, seems to be meditating. Feel as if we're in the waiting room at Doctor M's. Shank's on the phone for ages. Cheri's sitting in a wingback by the picture window. Her sleek shaved legs crossed, one foot swinging spells at Shank crouched beside the phone table. Practically has the thing tucked into his shirt, so private is this call.

The front door creaks open. Cheri pushes back into the chair like she's on a bad plane ride. Her eyes widen, waiting for those steps to come in. Through the French doors and into the living room walks Lacey, razor creased in one of his high fashion goon outfits. He eyes me and the Duke from up high there, won't lower his chin, it's business hours. He regards Cheri for some moments and then nods, gives her the creeps, her head jerks sideways. Lacey curls the corner of his mouth and enjoys Cheri's revulsion.

Shank's finally off the phone, stands next to Lace, both of them stare at us for a moment. They turn and go out into the narrow hall, talking low. Shank sticks his head back in, suddenly smiling red-faced insane.

"Hey, you two, c'mere. I got somethin to show you."

Cheri's lying back now, eyes closed, fingers at her temples.

"Now what," mutters the Duke as we get up to join them in the hall. Shank goes ahead, leading us down into the low, raw basement. The light flicks on, a guy I don't know too well is sitting there.

"You guys remember Murphy, eh?" asks Shank, his ringmaster hand displaying the guest of honour.

Murphy's bound to a wooden chair, stripped down. His shrivelled dick trying to hide between hairy thighs. A rag tied around his mouth, open sores on his face and chest, flab tits jiggling. Eyes big, not blinking at all, going back and forth between Shank and Lacey.

Shank dances around Murphy, squawking, arms flapping. A chicken strut, then a baboon scream, just can't contain himself. Lacey's shaking his head, breathes heavy, looks down his nose.

Murphy's rabbit eyes whip side to side trying to keep up with Shank. Shank's kissing him all over his grief swollen face, pinching that sad little prick. Shuddering, barking sounds from Murphy. Stink of backed up toilets, water all over the floor. Shank is sweating and alligator eyed, pawing at his own balls. Grabs a tool off the work bench, points it at us. Maniac howling, funny to him maybe.

But then I start laughing, going crazy, bent over crying, waving at Shank, trying to make him stop. He loves the encouragement. Sticks his tongue way out while holding the tool at his crotch like he's wacking off. Slobbering, weird throat noises. Murphy's sobbing and Lace is shifting his weight from foot to foot.

"The big time!" Shank hollers and goes boogey dancing up to Murphy, throwing his hips, making Hawaiian guitar sounds, feet way apart. Pokes Murphy with the tool, looks back at us. "Maybe I should shove this up his hole! Give him a good tune up!" He jumps into Murphy's lap,

52

bops up and down. "Not bad! I could get him stuffed!" More idiot laughter, breaking hard across the ears.

"Well," says Shank, tousling Murphy's hair. "My buddy here's in deep shit, eh, guys? What you think? His ol' lady's gotta come up with the bread or..." sucks his teeth, "we'll be mailing her back the only part she really wants!"

We're crowded into this one bulb cellar, stooping to fit in. Me and the Duke teary-eyed, out of breath. Murphy's heaving, weeping, tears and snot running down his face. 40 watt shadow belts across his pot belly, across his neck.

Shank stands up quick, turns to him. "Hey, buck up, old bean! That's no way to impress the boys!"

Murphy's got gray at his temples and gray in his bladder too, I bet. Got his wires crossed, really fucked up looks like. His eyes come up at us, blood shot and glazed, not even asking. Probably didn't realize when he crossed the tenuous line of friendship. Just stepped over it whistling to himself, cocky and shouting orders at everybody. Even Lace has a trace grin on him and I'm sitting on a pile of dusty beer cases, wiped out from the show.

But Shank gets bored fast. His new toy is boring already. Leans an elbow on Murphy's shoulder and gazes at him, wondering what other tricks he might know.

"Fuck it," he says finally, straightening up, "she'll come through. You're a lucky man, Murph. She loves yu a lot, I think. She'll come through with the bread, don't you worry. Besides, all this is your fault. Nobody fucks ME!" and he drives his heel into Murphy's foot.

A muffled yell and the gagged head slumps, moaning. Shank turns and goes up the stairs two at a time, calling back at us. "C'mon, let's have a drink."

Lacey shrugs at me, thumbs at Murphy. "Kid stuff," he grunts and waits for us to leave. He'll stay behind a minute, tighten up the harness, put Shank's guest to bed.

53

We're sitting on the back deck watching the sun go down. It does this every evening through the trees just for Shank. The man who would own Bay Street but chose instead to own himself.

Cheri brings out a tray of glasses and a bottle of Polish Vodka. As she sets it down on the white umbrella table, Shank slides his hand along the back of her bare thigh.

"You know, Nick," he says to me, a finger waving, thick jowls satisfied, "you and Stein did real good with Chops. Turned him over pronto, no fuckin around. And he's your pal..." Flat hand gesture, lips curled out, loaded pause. "I like that, no fuckin around..."

Shank savours those words, mixes them in with his imported booze, nods goodbye to the sun.

Cheri seems glad now, relieved, being sweet again. She's changed into a bright pink t-shirt dress. Putters about, makes our drinks, sits at Shank's feet, asks him what colour he wants the bathroom.

"I'm gonna give you guys a deal on the clean beige I got," Shank tells us. "Yeah, Nick, I like the job you did on Chops. It was very sincere... I'm gonna do you four points, what the hell, half a gram. You can have it for cost... No," he frowns, "put your money away, you can run a tab. Have another shot."

The Duke's looking around, content the world isn't hostile for a moment. It's not him down in the basement and this sunset is really strong, emotional. Lace is gone. Lying somewhere now in a coffin sized freezer, relaxing, checking the appointment book.

We're a faded photo, colours running. Me and the Duke sitting so rigid. Shank, casual as a jelly fish and Cheri bent over the tray putting more razor blades in our ice. Quiet creeping up around us like insects. We don't move a muscle, all staring into the heart of the sun.

"One other thing, Nick," says Shank, dipping a pinky into his drink.

"What is it?"

"You know Cabbagetown Mike?" he asks, licking the vodka from his finger.

"Yeah, I guess so."

"I hear he says he knows me, has a line through me."

"Seems like everybody knows everything these days."

Shank closes his eyes and rubs the bridge of his nose. "Yeah, it's a real drag nobody can keep straight no more."

11

>

Walking down Euclid from Shank's place I'm thinking about this Cabbagetown Mike guy he was fretting over. More low-rent bullshit that Shank can't seem to let go of.

The Duke is lagging behind, feeling around in his mouth, gingerly touching those bad teeth. Spits out a glob of bloody yellow slime then lets out a long burp, turning it into a kind of song.

"What about Cabbagetown Mike?" I ask, stopping to wait for him.

The Duke's cranking his jaw side to side, testing the rotting hinges. The aquiline features and rock star charm losing out badly. "It's Shank's own fault," he answers. "Still making room for these dipsticks. The thing is, though, if he's lettin us run a tab, he might hit on us to take care of it."

"I guess. But maybe we can do it easy. I heard this Mike guy's going off the deep end anyway."

"You know him?" asks the Duke.

"I know what he looks like."

"So we'll bury a suicide, is that it?"

I catch his eye, his tone. "Don't turn this around, Duke. The hook of it is that what we think means nothing. It's only how things turn out that counts. Anyway, Cabbagetown Mike's just some ass-fucked drifter who went through all the church missions before he made twenty. It doesn't matter who'll use the shovel on him."

The Duke's mouth tightens. He rest his knuckles on his hips and looks down at the pavement. "You don't have to lay it on for me, Nick. Just play your own deck."

→ → →

We're boneless in this wet blanket heat, still under the effects of inhaling a sample. Aimless amble over to Alexandra Park, two rippling mirages not moving closer nor further.

Kids splash about in the wading pool, sounding like a flock of excited birds. In the corner of the park, furthest from Bathurst Street, four or five homeless ragbags are sprawled out under the bushes, looking like World War I corpses. We stop for a park bench in the shade.

"This shit's nothin special," complains the Duke. "Still twists up your guts."

"Yeah, feels like pig tranquilizer," I say, slouching back.

He pulls out a loose smoke, feels his pockets for matches. "What you think about Big Time Murphy?" he laughs grimly, cupping his hands around a flame.

"Quite a show," I answer.

"A real dynamo," he says, offering me a drag. "The guy should be headlining in Vegas."

I take off my leather jacket, catch a bad gust of myself. Things feel suspended and nauseating. If I had a watch I'd throw it away.

The Duke is bent over, gacking up more ugly bone decay, letting it drop between his feet.

"You know what I hate?" he asks, wiping his mouth on the back of his hand.

"I dunno, losing the keys to the limo. How the hell would I know what you hate?"

"I'll tell you. I hate not living anywhere."

"You got a place to live."
"Yeah? Where?"

≋

We work our way back down to the neighbourhood through the back alleys, stop at the Seoul Variety for cut-rate American smokes and get a cup of take-out brake fluid from Frank's. Queen Street's blowing its wad. Credit mad bargain seekers wrestling over some one-of-a-kind gewgaw. Crushed to the wall by millionaire business refugees and Forest Hill fur coat junkies.

Covering our asses we retreat to Augusta Street and find Stein in his sunroom, sucking on limes, smoking cheap angel dust grass. We tell him what we saw up at Shank's.

"Big deal," he snorts. "That's penny ante stuff."

"Yeah," says the Duke, "till it happens to you."

"That'd never happen to me," replies Stein, giving him a bitter face. "I got other ideas."

He's in one of his spontaneous fevers, the man of the moment. Must have noticed the gray hairs today.

"What's up yur ass?" I jab at him.

"Nothin," he sulks. "I'm just sick of this. I gotta get outa this scene. Nothin ever happens."

The Duke doesn't get it. "So?"

Stein's outraged, leaps to his feet, arms waving. "So?! Waddaya mean so?! So like I wanna make some money so I never gotta see you bastards again!"

He's got the cold sweat, only bad pot around and broke. No fronts and no more borrow, sorry. The regular broads he'd been hitting on are stonewalling him and he's too jangled to consider a B&E. No time, anyway. Hands bad shake and grinding teeth.

"Jesus, Stein," I mutter at him. "I didn't know you were so bad."

"Fuck you, *Nikos*," he spits at me. "I'm on top of it. Don't worry about me. Look at yurself."

It brings out the sinner in all of us. And the lord spake to him. Public opinion told Stein to make the big move. Get on the fast track. Shake, go, get it. Business, that's it. He got wound up and slicked down. Tough, payroll busting son of a bitch. Found a few ulcers, bought a ton of porn. Three suits and two pairs of shoes, kept one eye on the land flip market. Stein did a lot of soul searching.

"I gotta find somethin people want. Somethin that fits into their lifestyles. Enough of you guys, enough of this. I'm movin up."

"Great, Stein, just remember your roots."

"Roots? Oh, yeah? Go fuck yourself."

So with massive guaranteed World Bank loans Stein set out on foot to find the fallen hem in the fabric of society. Scurrying under the fence, gladhanding all the way. Inviting clients into a refridgerator-box office and passing out rubber business cards.

And he levers his way into the market. Finds a niche, an oily fracture to slither into. A string wart vendor and high-commission attitude salesman. Expands his line and opens an exclusive club where networking powerheads from Bay Street megabanks can really relax. Let their hair down and immerse themselves in their ancient heritage.

The cream of the transnational boardrooms. A high flying CEO. Trembling, booze-coked decision-maker getting his ass burned on the TSE, feeling that hard pressure from Tokyo. Sensing another impending attack of angina, he throws the Yonge Street leather gear into the snake-skin briefcase and heads for Stein's psychic balancing parlour. Slipping the gold American Excess card to a retired porn star at the door and mumbling, "Whatever it takes...", our old boy can finally sit alone in one of the darkened booths with a one-way mirror window, getting his rocks off while anonymously

59

watching a pair of twelve year-old boys 69 each other. A trusted member of the bottom line gang, balls trussed up to his neck in custom harness, black dildo jammed up the ass, very privately entertained. Growling, cursing, spitting on sacred Catholic texts.

"Mr. Stein, you give *good* business."

"This con is gonna make a bundle," Stein beams, "you'll see. And listen, fellas, I forgive yuz for doubtin me. Once it gets off the ground, you're both in."

"Really? Man, you're alright. You know that?"

If anybody came down on him for doing this kind of thing, Stein dismissed them easily.

"C'mon," he'd say, "it's only a bit of stress relief for the pinstripes. Besides, if anything is gonna save this bullshit economy, it's the service sector."

That made the experts stop and think.

"Anyhow," he'd tell them, "these johns can fuck themselves with running chainsaws for all I care. As long as they keep their mitts off the kids, it's not my business. Hell, don't you believe in human rights?! I got these punks in a volume wholesale deal outa the slums of Saigon from the Minister of Immigration herself. Doncha know what's going on in the third world, man?! They'd be dead in a toxic waste filled ditch if I didn't save them! But then all you sandal wearers get on my back... It's never easy trying to help people..."

Stein found out the hard way. Nobody wants any help these days. He was out of business in about five minutes.

"Face it," I'm consoling him. "Your ideas are too far ahead, too advanced. Know what I mean?"

"Sure. You pricks. It was you and your bad vibes that screwed me up!"

I couldn't believe he was trying to pin this thing on me. "Hey, it's not my fault you're too goddamn ignorant to know the difference between a poll and a pole!"

We're both on our feet suddenly, circling each other, balls forward, hollering like horny rednecks. Stein flicks a lit cigarette off my chest and booms: "If you're such a brain, fuckface, how come you haven't cashed in?! Still cornholing old douchebags to go through the purse!"

That was below the belt. I grab him, pull him close. "You want real trouble?" I ask quietly, an inch from his face. "I'll give you the wettest tongue job this side of a ten year-old slant whore. My rep is shot and I got the plague, right? I couldn't care less, man..."

Stein goes pale. Sweating upper lip quavers, his eyes shift anxiously. "Okay, relax," he whispers, backing away, "take it easy, no problem." His hands go up in a gesture of good faith. "Loosen up, Nick... Everything's fine."

That doesn't cut it, I bear down on him. "We were supposed to stick together, man, remember?"

Stein's embarrassed now, ashamed. "Yeah, I know," he says meekly, turning away. "I just thought..."

"What?!"

"Nothin..." he blubbers.

"*Nothin* is right!"

He looks back at me. His face a hunted, exhausted thing. "But... I see what's going on in this town and..."

I grab his hair, twisting hard, watch him grit his teeth with pain but hardly resisting.

"This is Toronto!" I yell at him. "It's clean, it's safe and it's world class! Exactly what guys like us need!"

Stein slumps, a broken man. The Duke is standing beside me, shaking his head, pats me on the back.

"Well," he sighs, "Stein's lucky to have a few real friends left." He pulls out the rest of the score we got off Shank and cocks his head at me. "It's not the good stuff, but it oughta bring around Mr. Megabucks here."

"We never get the good stuff," I tell him.

The Duke's eyebrows lift and he nods tiredly.

"No, we don't."

61

12

SF, slim, mature, unattached, outgoing,
professionally oriented, environmentally
active, loves laughter, wide interests in
arts and travel, seeks suitable
companion.

She is an old douchebag, it's true.

Think she was looking for a way out of her old man
the night she kept lingering near me, encouraging my
drunk. Her hands, kind of big for a woman, all over my
back. Short-nailed fingers wrapping through my ribs,
grabbing my ass, smiling like she was ahead of herself.
Funnier than hell to her she'd be doing this sort of thing.

It was at a magazine launching at one of those gallery
deals on Lower Spadina. Fussy little food on the buffet
table, some hard thinking going on up on the walls. I end
up there by scamming an invite to get at the free booze,
trying to cozy up to the alternative establishment.

The place is jammed with a lot of semi-nobodies and
never-was-beens. Local yokel art critics and media flakes.
The women looking mostly like hep methodist zealots
and the men a mixture of avant-garde hobbyists and
pathologically fashionable mutes. It's a stiff, mostly

WASP crowd, pumped up with government money. A few grain-fed ethnix stirred in to add a dash of flavour.

Didn't get much attention till this 40ish arts-admin type starts up with me. Expensively dressed in low-key solid colours, a bony Anglo grace. Could be my big break. But her laughter is something withdrawn, distracted. Pale eyes meeting my shape and size. She asks if I'm an artist.

Yeah, of course I'm an artist. I'm in a band. You know.

Ridiculous the way these things start out. We're at her place later and she's shy but matter-of-fact. Another proposal to appraise. Translucent, blue skin reflecting corpse white as silk shirt parts and each article of clothing is handled with finger-tips. Not a bad bod for her age, not that I'm one to talk. But still, I'm not blind.

We're drinking some of her quality booze and she rolls up a bill for the lines I'm laying down. Jockeying for position on the couch, my hands moving over plains and curves, judging her size and proportions. Weighing the odds on a triple-beam balance. I'm thinking about the bedroom, wondering how it looks, smells. I guess she cleaned it up before coming out tonight, knowing or hoping she'd bring something back. The living room is tasteful, minimal, polite. She's asking me all the unique stuff.

"Have you ever slept with another man?"

Yeah, sure, in parks, in ditches, on floors, passing out cold wherever the mood strikes... Slept with another man...

In this low intoxicated light I'm seeing right through her ice skin. Under that skin is a body, her whole body ravaged. Tits sagging, stretch marks around her hips and ass. Her sick hide, sick of having to live out each day to its end. Every inch of her covered in the scrawled out lists and priorities of another year.

She looks at me in this formal way. Keeps pulling her eyes off, lets them roam around the room, at random

63

over her objects. We're silent in this cozy nest. This scene the Duke really begs for. The clean angle kitchen. Mail, subscriber magazines, credit card bills on a narrow table by the door. The above store old place, all fixed up. Flat white latex, original art. It's called a life.

Everything must hold a sacred station and we're off the black canvas couch. She's topless, I'm bottomless and she turns on a dim bulb in the bedroom. The futon and refinished dresser. Yeah, clean, ready for me. Lights, camera, I'll strap on the bridle.

She goes into the can whispering to herself and she's in there for a long time. I get undressed, lying in her bed, waiting, my hand idly playing with a soft cock.

She's in there thinking. She's thinking: What am I doing? Who is this guy? I'm impaired. Why did I bring him back here? How do I get rid of him? What did he say his name is? Do I want to fuck him? He doesn't give bad face, anyway.

Yeah, so gimme a chance and see what I can do, lady. You haven't even seen my routine yet. Leave this reading light on so you can look up at my face. It's gonna be so sweet. Young, they tell me, when I'm into it. We should get to know each other. It doesn't have to be just this. I'm not such a heartless pig. I don't live only for my hard-on. This could take a couple of weeks. We'll have lunches and a few movies. Go to out of the way bars where we don't have to get into each other's friends or hang-outs. Lemme walk out of here tomorrow with a little dignity, y'know? So I can meet the crew and yap to them about how set up you are and how far I'll be able to string you. They can nod their heads and appreciate my strong instincts. Why doncha gimme a hundred dollar bill I can show them? Really get on top of the conversation, shut them up for a minute. What's it to you?

64

We start going at it broken down, a car that won't start. The cheap rubber I'm wearing squeaking and mashing. She keeps her eyes on something behind my head. I feel as if I'm chopping wood and it gets so we're both thinking of things to be done and *what time is it?* Our eyes closed, very near. Lips sucking on one another and she's composing the letter she's going to write to the guy she married and ended up tossing out.

I cum before she's even warm.

She sits up, pushing her brown hair out of the way and stares at the broken condom hanging off the end of my dick. I watch her run a finger up her cunt and then absentmindedly wipe the glistening sperm along her thigh.

She gets up for work before eight. In the shower and out and dressing and touch of make-up. Rushing around, throwing last night's underwear in the hamper, distracted, checking the date book, talking to me and I'm not listening.

"Think you can lend me some money?" I ask.

"How much?"

"I dunno, fifty?"

"Well, I can give you forty now..."

What are you saying? I'm supposed to come back for the other ten?

She's nervous and in a big hurry, hedging around about me going and I'm waiting it out, see what she does with all the practical advice crammed into her head. What the hell is wrong with you? You forget the moral imperatives you learned at those self-help workshops? So much for all that magazine research declaring you've really got things figured out.

"Here," she says, putting the money on the bed. "I've got to go. Call me later if you like."

Give her a groggy put on, reassure by touching her I

won't sell all the furniture once she's left. Wants to trust me maybe, but keeps looking down my leather and boots and all the cheap tin garbage I wear. The jolly rodger.

Kiss good-bye, nothing long and wet, just this dry lip, squeeze of the arm. But she turns at the bedroom door, gives me a wicked face, her hand caressing her tit. Maybe impressed with her own irreverence, maybe giving me something to get anxious about.

That should keep him close.

Hardly worth the trouble for the forty bucks I got out of her and scoffing a bottle of the same wine we drank on the couch. But not a bad guy. Left her a note and took her phone number. Pried through her photos and letters in the bedroom desk. A husband somewhere. Lost, divorced, auctioned off. Mothers, fathers, sisters, big family. *My family is very important to me.*

I get this choking in the kitchen just hearing the clock and the traffic out in the morning. Feel my face, it's wet. I can't believe it. Where'd she go? Why this now? She didn't really have to go anywhere. She's probably down in her car, smoking, waiting for me leave. Went and got a take out coffee and the paper, is giving me a half hour or so. She'll come back, I'll still be here. She'll tell me she forgot something, maybe I want a ride?

✖

Finally leave. Look both ways down the street. For a second I don't recognize a thing. A lot of commuter geeks coming east on Queen from the highway, from Mississauga. Guys my own age with condos and cars and moustaches and white shirts from Simpson's. I begin walking west, they all stare grimly from behind their windshields. They know where I been, what I've been up to. They smell it right through the aftershave and

66

hysterical morning radio, right past the sunshine girl.

I get to Rooneem's Bakery and wait. Drink coffee for almost three hours before Stein shows up with Chops.

"You could be into somethin good," warns Stein. "Don't fuck it up right away."

I'm emphatic. "Aw, no way. She's got a new Nissan SX with a sunroof and some good booze at home."

"What's she do?"

"Big deal art job at the OAC. Good money."

Chops is lapping this up, cat milk for him. "An older woman with money," he sighs. "Nicky, it doesn't get any better..."

⊥⊥⊥

Saw her again in the evening. Bored, I go by saying, "I don't know what I'm doing here but I just wanted to see you and I'll take off if you're busy."

"No, no," she replies, "come in, I'm glad to see you. I've been thinking about you today."

Sure, been writing me love letters I bet. Truth is, I find you very beautiful standing there in the living room with the plants and glass coffee table. The way you suit those Italian flats and the big cotton skirt hiding your wide ass.

You are from a good white family. A Rosedale girl maybe, Jarvis Collegiate grad. You have a life, right? Friends, other women you care about?

I really enjoy the way you always push your hair back from your face. A slim hand running up your forehead, pushing the hair straight over the back and falls again and again to the side over one eye. Eyes always at the floor and coming up in glances.

I came back since maybe I do want to talk. More than just the quirked semi-private, semi-brainless nonsense you seem to want to hear. Dirty smart talk talking smart and dirty. Yes, ma'am, you have tapped into the flipside.

I'll give you the indifferent distance that makes you come to me. Here, I'll give you some right now. Taking our skins right off. Walk across an ocean of broken glass to get to you. Listening for that gasp. Your eyes closed, lying under the street lights. I can see your age in your neck, lines across the throat. Two candles burning at the bedposts above your head. Your naked white ass on a green meadow. We rock, a perfectly balanced wooden horse.

I think about being a person with you. Being older and straighter with you. How we'd have kids, dogs, cars and summer houses. Go to parties, get ready for those parties. Your perfume and earrings. Know you through your clothes, your record collection, your books, your handwriting. Think about us at dinner with friends, with family. It'd be a fine world like that. In ten thousand apartments right this minute we're made of love. Cutting holes in calendars, crossing out birthdays. We're getting to work late, daydreaming out the window. Forgetting to pay the bills and giving head in the car on the Don Valley Parkway. Drinking till the bottle breaks. Always horny around me now, it makes you walk different, tell me to fuck off a lot.

Shut up, c'mere...

On the kitchen chair with your knees pulled up, mouth hung open, hands pushing hard down on my head. I got a hold of you in my mouth, you came falling, I caught you in my mouth. This beautiful mouth with rose red lips. Balanced you so easily on the tip of my tongue, held you in my teeth. Your clit learns to love me and gets resentful when any pretender tries to chat it up. I piss you off when I can. Not call, not show up. Find me drunk in the Cameron, mindless, happy to see you. Trying to grab your sleeve, you pull away. It's alright, let everyone here see us. These people all know me, this only helps.

She sits next to me, annoyed, has a drink. All cross-legged, hands in your lap, smoking deeply, ignoring me and I'm trying to get my fingers between your thighs.

Don't. You're such an asshole.

How about your asshole? Does it miss me?

She gets up to leave. I must be insane.

Don't go, c'mon, I was just having fun... I don't wanna go home tonight and I wouldn't mind going for a drive.

I have to come up with some crippled line. We're at the door then outside talking slow confessions. I get my arms around her, pick her right up, carry her behind the bar and into the lane. She's acting put upon, intolerant, but then shoving me up against the wall, grabbing my hair in both hands real tight just wanting me, my mouth, grinding her hips, trying to jam a knee up between my legs. This woman right now is shattered through each dissected cliché. Exploded, all hung up on each other's plumbing, laying those stories to waste.

I came a long way west to find you.

●

She lets me drive, curls up next to me. Yeah, yeah...you're the baby girl. The skinny pixie little thing. Mischievous fingers crawling in your mouth. Okay, get out the hoolahoops and take that doll's clothes off. We'll gather up brown leaves in the autumn park to draw out the lines of our dream home and your bicycle will be a horse and mine a motorcycle. And you know, it wasn't your age that drove me away, it was the hint you've got another life. But that's not the point, is it? I didn't come into you and your bed to hear this.

Your hand on my shoulder. "You okay?"

Don't look so worried. In a few months we'll ignore each other in the street.

∇±∇

The old bag isn't around and I'm making myself sick thinking about her. I consider sitting on her steps and waiting. Loitering in the street below her place, feeling strung, pretending to wait for the streetcar.

But, hey, c'mon! I'm the rebel rocker! Yeah, the cuntfuckin cocksucker! I got time on my hands and shit on my shoes! Figure it out, buddy boy...

I go over to the Black Bull looking for Cassandra but she's not around either and all I want is to find a way out of going home tonight. It's still early, I tell myself. Relax, man. You got four hours or so till last call and then the speaks. Hey, fella, you got all night to never go home.

End up walking west all the way over to Shaw Street, near the nuthouse. Panting cur almost running. I wanna get to that Peroxide job I met at the speak on Liberty. Get there before she goes out. Hoping she's got the good sense not go out before 11. Turning the corner north from Queen I see her sitting on the broken down porch steps with one of the roomies. All this *what am I doing here?* running through my head. I'm stopped, she sees me. This curious, cautious twist to her face. Some small talk.

"Was just passin by, what's happenin?"

She's got these unsure movements I didn't notice the time we ended up here. A recovering zombie, maybe on trancs.

"I'm doing my hair tonight," she tells me.

"No kidding? What colour is your hair, anyway?"

"Blonde, just like this. But I dye it. I do it for you."

"For me?"

"Yeah. You wanted proof? This is proof."

"I see it."

"No you don't. Come closer. Let's see what your side of the coin looks like, sugar..."

"You're a miserable cunt."

"Makes you hard, uh?"

70

13

My fate to always end up with a dog faced baboon who's too stupid to have a bank account. Did it my way. Yeah, I'm the kennel keeper. I've got a horde of hyenas and banshees and wailing coyotes. Every screeching nitwit who wants some real attention will eventually find my doorstep.

It even pisses off the Duke. Gets all wrought up over it. Can't stand to see this waste of good flesh on me.

"For a guy who doesn't like women..." he says, his voice trailing off.

We're idling dumbly down Queen Street, making low sucking noises, shoving each other, checking out the tide of lips, legs, hairdoos. But in the washed out background, through the rush of hard hype thoroughbreds there's something not quite right. A guilty reek caught in the seams of success. Back there, shrinking from the sunlight, the battle weary sister, a wasteland of social criticism and theoretical wars. She silently begs change from the doorway, surrounded by her machine-gun nest of over-stuffed plastic bags and five layers of old coats. Trotted out every winter by the tv news. Toothless and friendly, a flaccid lesson shown to troublesome kids. This ugly old witch climbing out of the sewer grating to reclaim her post when the shops close down.

She used to have a name and a picture of herself in a print dress, standing in a St. Thomas tobacco field. She once knew a man who owned a car. He'd told her she was good with a dollar so she'd know not to expect things to start out big. Making bread out of old socks, darning scalps back together, she'd had the cleanest toilet in the land.

With the pensions coming regular things were looking up after all the small-helping years. The new sofa had been paid off for months and even the tv was practically in the clear. But her old man, well, he had a burning thing in his guts that put him off work and even driving, and he'd never told her the bank owned the house.

Still, she nursed him. When he lay there barfing up his lungs, avoiding his debts by dying, she nursed him like a baby. For nearly fifty years he'd beaten her into a crude image of his own lost self and now he was leaving her with only a pan full of phlegm. But yet she held him in her arms and told him bed time stories while he lay dead for two days or more.

Crazy old bag, went nuts. Neighbours heard her wailing late one night and called the city. So the wagon pulled up to the three room shack, took away the old man's carcass and dragged her down to the shelter.

"Don't worry," the caseworker told the circle of nosey neighbours, gawking in their bathrobes and slippers, "she's no harm. We'll slot her into one of those new low-income developments going up and she's got a sister-in-law listed as next of kin."

But the subsidized apartment was twice her pension cheque, the sister-in-law had died the same year the Leafs last won the Stanley Cup and nobody knew where the jailbird son was parked.

Anyway, she was nothing but trouble at the shelter. Fussing, crying, wouldn't talk. Kept wandering off, thinking the old man was down at the draft hall and

72

she'd better get home to make his supper. Night time beer prices would be kicking in soon and he'd be coming stagger piss up the alley down his pants, gob on his sleeve, snot hanging out and yelling at cars.

"Didju fight in the war?!" His snarling head rolling around at me and the Duke at the corner of Queen and Palmerston.

"I fought in the fuckin war!" he sprays all over us. "You know what's wrong with youz?"

"No, what?"

"You're fulla shit queers! Haw haw haw..."

"Yeah?"

"Yeah, I know. I'm a veteran. King's Own Rifle. You two pukes ever been to France? Pairee?"

"No."

"Good whewrs, eh? Those little Frenchies was starvin when we shows up. Keerist! They'd fuck yu till yu drop fur jist a brandy. Good brandy in them joints."

"Yeah?"

"Goddamn right. You friggin nothins don't know about women. Treatin em all like the Queen. You think they're all *ladies?*"

"Ladies?"

"Most of em is whewrs. Yu don't get ladies around every day, y'know!"

He's right. You don't get many ladies anymore. They stopped making them. The plant shut down when the Japs undercut the market. Everybody got layed off and now we've got to import ladies from far away places.

"Fuckin wino," the Duke grumbles, still staring up the road at this guy stumbling along after his sermon.

"He's not a wino," I say. "I know where he lives."

"What?"

"He lives with this old bag in one of those shacks on Robinson. I seen him when he's sober. Not a bad guy really."

73

"France..." the Duke mutters. "*I've* never been to fuckin France."

"Forget about France," I keep on. "Whores are the same everywhere now."

"Whores..." This whole thing has him depressed. "They all end up crates of shit," he gripes. "We're gonna wind up like that asshole. There's no gettin away from it. Being like that comes naturally to most people."

This is the kind of crap the Duke gets into when there's less than twenty bucks between us. The world goes philosophical without money. It drives us up to Shank's place, moth eaten lemmings down the grease slide.

Ω

We get let in by this creep with a woodpecker hair cut. Shank's in the kitchen yelling at Cheri. From down the hall I can see her looking up at him. He's got her pushed down into a wooden chair, her hands flat on her thighs. She's wearing canary yellow big shorts and a *Green The World* t-shirt.

"It didn't happen!" Cheri's crying. Tears and head turning away. Drape of that sunny blonde down her neck.

Shank grabs her head with both hands, foaming psychotic's justice. "Open yur mouth!" he's yelling. "Do it, you cunt!"

Cheri's struggling, Shank's forcing her jaw open, two banana fingers trying to jam a hundred dollar bill down her throat.

"I didn't touch him!" she's pleading, choking.

"Eat it, you pig! It's what you want! Eat it!"

He wrestles her onto the floor, straddles her chest. See him from behind, the fat back packed into a powder blue shirt. Both hands in her face below him. Her legs kicking, she's gagging, begging.

Shank finally eases off, gets up slowly, the fever

subsiding. Grabs Cheri up like a drunk, shoves her down the hall at us. "Go upstairs!"

She runs past, make-up flooded face, red slap marks on her. Goes crying up the stairs, arms holding each other.

Shank's still breathing hard, wiping his head with a dish towel. Sits in the chair, sighs heavily and lights a smoke.

The Duke gives me a smarmy look, tipping his head toward Shank who's still in some heat. "Hey, boss," he taunts, "everythin gonna be okay?"

"Yeah, just beautiful," Shank answers as he gets up and comes past us into the living room. "C'mere," he says, "I wanna show you guys something."

"Not again," I murmur.

Shank's messing with the VCR. Shuffles through a bunch of tapes before sticking one in the machine. We sit on the couch three abreast. The peckerhead who let us in stands to the side, arms crossed, all on one hip, in that frowning fag way. Sound critical judgement.

The tape comes on. It's a home movie of Shank and Cheri. Spinning camera, grainy dark then bright white. Cheri's undressing slowly, soundless, in a stripper put on that's her lips moving up to the lens out of focus so hand and bra with hair hanging down mouth enveloping a purple pillar covering then pushing up tits bare tan line ass orange blue colours blur up close sudden to face down in a meat freezer full of

"What's that?" asks the Duke.

"Her rosette," replies Shank.

"Her rosette?"

"Yeah."

And static covered Cheri laughing like a Lebanese hostage: *I'm having a good time, Mom and Dad. They're treating me real good and don't worry but just*

Shank hits the remote and the frame freezes. Cheri's colour burst lips super close up.

"That's some nice footage," mugs the Duke.

"Not bad," allows Shank, staring at the screen. "Chris here shot it."

Chris Peckerhead gives us a condescending little smirk, lightly brushes the bangs from his face and goes off into the kitchen.

"He's queer," says Shank. "But he's alright."

"Yeah," I add, "Cheri looks great."

"She's okay, I guess," he squirms in a sympathetic way. "Just gets outa her pants once in a while..."

Shank's flopped out on the couch, head back, whimsical. The tape has put him in good spirits. He tumbles to the floor doing a spastic sort of athletic manoeuvre, sommersaulting to his feet. Feelin frisky, feeling awright! Git it on, brother! He's wacking us on the backs, dancing around, play-boxing.

"You two are lucky," Shank tells us, shutting off the machine. "You don't have some chick to take care of. Just the good life, eh, boys? On your own. That's the way to do it."

"You still got Murphy sittin around downstairs?" I ask him as we move toward the kitchen.

"Who?" Mock stupid, hand cupped to his ear. "Murphy! Haw! That was funny!" Shank's gleeful, doing his hunchbacked twirl. "His old lady paid up but he enjoyed his stay. I got him on the video, he was beeyooteefool! Chris put the nice make-up on him. Yeah... Murphy was funny..."

Shank's blabbering away as I watch him break up some rock and put it in a black ivory pipe full of ash. The Duke deftly steps into this drivel like a waltz artist. "Hey, Shank" he schmoozes, "how 'bout sprinkling a couple grains on that."

Shank's face starts this happy scold. "You guys got no class. I don't go for that kinda shitheel stew. Anyway, better take what you can get."

76

What can I get? I can get a kidney failure and maybe some vague withdrawl symptoms. Bad skin I've already got, not to mention this oozing piss infection I picked up from one of those bulldogs in Kensington market. I wouldn't mind a running toothache, a bladder problem is on order and manic depression is standard equipment. You got a catalogue I can look at?

The peckerhead is chattering to the Duke and pulling out an envelope of 8x10 glossies. The Duke's eyeing them with sober assessment and the geek's hands are flapping away.

"Well," the peckerhead explains, "I now design exclusively in leather and three stores on Queen West are *very* interested. These *are* works of art after all."

I glance down at shots of this belt harness crap. Pictures of lithe youngsters in modern jazz poses with sucked in faces and gracious arms. Up on their toes, naked but for these handcrafted, totally unique in the universe leather diapers. 18 year-olds who escaped from Ottawa or Windsor or The Soo and came in search of the golden butt plug. Future fisting champions working out their routine before heading off to a waitering job in New York.

"That's a nice belt," the peckerhead points, his other hand on the standard hip.

"Yeah," I say, "I had it made. I like these studs."

"They're rivets actually."

The Duke's giving me the loose eyeball while Chris, my new friend, is checking out my belt, me, my crotch. Already rolling the head of my cock around in his mouth, his asshole the undulating lips of a catfish.

Shank's watching, getting ideas, getting excited, feeling himself up. Hoping his latest purchase is gonna live up to the sales pitch.

14

■

"Man, you believe how beautiful she is?"

Stein's incinerated by this Bishop Strachan fantasy we're sizing up. Across the way and new in the bar.

"I'd love to do her," agrees the Duke, in a trance.

"Do her?" Stein's incredulous. "Man, I'd let her shit in my mouth."

Sure, she'd squat over it so pretty. Peaches and cream school girl dream wrapped in a tartan kilt. The guy with her's some gomer who's been showing up for the past while and now he's bringing around this piece. Hey, friend, what is she, your sister? What's her shoe size? The three of us get queasy when her eyes sweep by, passing us over, abandoned roadside wrecks.

The Duke's first to our defense. "Look at her," he says. "Some MP's daughter. You gotta be one of those pool playing accountants from the Squeal Club if you wanna stamp her."

Stein's not into the interference. "How would you know?" he argues, licking his lips. "What a body..."

Body body. Not one of these demented dyke torsos that turn you right off skin. No, this is a real virgin belly. Tits with their own personalities. Those legs, back breaking flying head scissors, the whole deal. Get her hot and you're boiled, son.

"Stein," I tell him. "That baby would go through you like a blender, man. Dead of a heat failure. Nuts burstin and there's Stein in the garbage can, tongue hangin out."

"Think you're funny, Nick?" he snaps at me. "I've had better than her, man! I used to be a real cute guy!"

How cute? Cute enough to say: yes, my child, come with me now, slide into the car. It's the leather seats which smell so rich. I see your thigh next to me from the driver's seat. Exposed thigh which I will defend until the weekend is over.

But it all turns the poor guy to grief. Stein can't deny she might as well be on another planet. "Women," he sours. "I'm sick of women. There's no point, anyway... What the hell could I tell her? She wouldn't understand anything."

"Take it easy, Stein," the Duke strokes him. "Don't get down. You just ain't met the *right* woman."

We'll wait for her, she'll be there one day, for all of us. Moon goddess, earth goddess, sea nymph. Fuck-faced sister of a sucking chest wound in my bed and never ever leave our fairy tale land of incest. In a million schmaltzy music videos, we'll live heart to heart and I'll protect you from all boredom, old age. I will become the older man you've been neurotically craving since first bleed. I'll become senile, sick and dead, all while your nipples are still facing up. That's the ticket, my love. I've got it all mapped out for you. Your beauty and genius will not go to waste because, as if you didn't know, you have every right to live under the weight of my hopeless ambitions. The right to bear our stillborn children who would have turned out necrophiliacs. The right to cook me that poison you call food. Yes, you'll be left a wealthy and powerful widow. So listen, sh...shut up a minute...this is the devotion you were going on about.

≅

"Hey, there's your old crow."

The Duke picks you out standing by the door. Somehow bored, looking irritated to be here. A man's suit jacket on. Your big hands shoved way deep into the pockets. Push back hair, push back and smoking smoke. Reluctantly sitting with us, knowing you're cutting yourself down for this. Putting us on all over your skin, pain lotion. Suffering from your own stupid underestimations.

When I bound your wrists in a perfect X and took a picture, the value of that act was not lost on me and I don't even read. I knew you'd bloom sooner or later and I wasn't surprised it was sooner. Kept us together a long while, didn't it? Longer than any of the horoscopes predicted. We decimated your bank accounts and exhausted your plastic. You haven't been shopping in ages and we missed that film festival party last week. All dressed up to go but start necking in the bathroom and later and later. Smoking pinheads of junk to stay calm, we never left the parking spot. I'm scraping out the bottom of your purse early on a Sunday morning. You hear the zipper slowly open, creaking steps of mine shuffle shuffle through the wallet, ID, credit cards, phone book, booth photo of us. Hand shadows quietly sliding out bills and bigger change. Sorry, I wanna take out my Peroxide plum and see if her roots have grown in. Looking back into the bedroom for a second to see you curled under the sheet and know you're awake.

Is he gone yet? Door silently shuts and the sun breaks through to you. Calls your name, tells you you're next. From today on, from this day on. Haven't plucked your eyebrows for so long, look at these nails. God, nic stains, a vein throbbing in your forehead, eyes sucked in by your brain emptying out. Must be this bright bathroom light.

15

♠

Wake up to a Monday noon in Cassandra's phone booth room at the Black Bull Hotel. Peer into the tin mirror hanging next to her bed. Hey, how's it going raccoon eyes? Have a good time last night? Yeah, great. Fuck off.

Cassandra's already up and strapped in tight, steel belted, got her five layers of make-up on. Sitting at the end of the bed, the bush of wild streaked hair down her back. Strumming the unplugged stratocaster copy and singing in a low, rumbling voice of doom, of angels, of abject nonsense.

I grope through her mound of rags trying to recognize my stuff, needing a smoke. She sings a ballad of how I come running back to her after every infatuated disaster. Her lament backed up by the muted thud of the juke box in the bar beneath her room.

We often lie in her narrow bed and talk about them, these women. Cassandra wanting all the details, keeping a list of symptoms, making them lyrical. Comparing me to her four or eight or how many husbands. Each of them cutting her throat for loving too much. And she never shuts her mouth about all these semi-exboyfriends. Going back and forth crazy about how I stab her in the back and forget her for every fifty dollar skirt who comes by. And I got to jerk her off before sticking it in cuz she don't get off on the penetration so good. She likes it, or so she says. But to get the rush, it's gotta be by hand, hand delivered. Sign here, Cassandra, and don't forget to tip me or I won't be coming back.

"I saw you leaving that woman's place," she says coldly.

"Yeah? Fallin head first down the stairs into your trash can no doubt."

See, you must remember, Cassandra, that's a serious and meaningful and incomprehensible relationship. You and me, we're both too dim to mess things up all that bad. Every straight I know or grew up with looks at you and gets all grossed out.

"You fuck *her?!*"

"Sure I fuck her," I tell them. "Why not? I ain't gonna be buried with her. I'm only fuckin her."

The Duke figures I oughta be your agent, really get you off the ground. Run you like a personal computer. He tells me not to tell Stein.

"Listen, Nick, whatever you do, don't let him in on it. You know Stein and the venture capital business. Like shit'n'sugar."

"Yeah, yeah," I put him off, "I won't forget."

"No, really," he's insisting. "With her talent? If you get her head cleaned out, it's easy street. You saw her in the back room at the Cameron. She shut those morons up good. You think any of these brainless sluts with albums out are any better? We're talkin *money.*"

"Why don't you do it then?" I ask him.

"Naw, naw..." he replies, holding up his palm. "It's you she's hung up on."

"Yeah, sure, like a coat rack."

The three of us sitting in Rooneem's. Holding a table between a potato-schnozed Slav and a pair of day-pass lunatics. The CIA acid experiment busboy hovers around us, worshipping Cassandra, yabbering about her Queen of Sheba get up. Fuck, I'm a conservative guy, getting too old for this freak show. Yeah, right, it's a popped culture. We'll make a fortune in one afternoon. How long can a guy last in this skinny-assed pose?

"Yep, this one's really the ticket," the Duke confides to me. "Get her a few warm-up gigs and it's top of the video charts next week."

"Maybe you're right," I'm whining. "But I'm the one who's gotta keep at her."

"That's okay," he purrs, good natured guy, "you ain't found big momma yet, have yu?"

"Thanks, thanks a lot, man..."

Stein stumbles through the door, in the grip of some paranoid PCP grass, saying "what?" a lot and fighting his way out of an undersized sports-jacket. But there's no keeping this good man down. Business is his business and he joins our conference.

"This is it," he tells us, clearing the table with a dramatic swipe. "First, she needs a new wardrobe. She's gotta be properly sold. This street's gotta be blown apart."

"I don't wanna look like Elizabeth Taylor!" Cassandra starts crying.

Stein's adament, inflating his chest. "Let me tell you!" he shouts. "I was on Queen Street before any of these pony-tailed fascists! Before the boutiques and blackout shops! Before the Chinese and WASP kids got their high priced hair-cuts down here! Before all the bars on this strip were beer commercial sets! I was here when there was only toilet seats and old lady girdles in them windows! Bread was thirty-two cents!" He glances about quickly. "Hey! Where's the LiveEyeDiscoTVcam?! I wanna see myself on the news tonight!"

83

16
Ø

"What's to worry about? Just stand him a good wack outa what I gave yu and take him for a ride. Put yur heads together, you'll figure it out. Anyway, you guys are in deep with me. It's not like you're doing me a favour..."

So, Cabbagetown Mike, the bigmouthed lightweight finally ran outa credit. Went to sit down one day and the chair gets kicked out from under him. Falls backwards, keeps falling. Surprised to look up at a circle dome of fish eyes staring down.

Set us free, we three men of orient time. On Highway 7, somewhere before dawn. Factory outback of the city, flat for miles, land with salt driven through it. In a borrowed '82 Malibu, swigging cheap scotch, waiting for Mike to take the vomit comet.

Stein at the wheel, gunning down a straightaway. His eyes rapid around the rearview, smoking like the devil. The Duke's in the back seat with Mike, taking in the sights.

"Man," Mike's whispering, "this is clean..."

I look around at him. Head lolling, dog in the back window. His hands are open, turned up in his lap, eyes slits, lips hanging loosely.

"What the fuck, man?" says Stein, shooting me a crazed look. "We gonna drive around all night waitin for this goof to kick? We shoulda taken him back to his room."

"Shut up," I tell him. "Like I said, his chick woulda been back from work."

"C'mon," he's bitching at me, "do somethin."

"What am I supposed do?"

"I dunno," Stein answers, gripping the wheel and leaning forward. "I don't want him puking in the car. I gotta get it back."

I'm chewing down my fingers, watching the highbeams path. Turn around to Mike again. Shades of night move quickly over him. Through the rear window, the highway looks as black as an open mouth. Sounds like Mike's humming to himself when I finally reach for the handle and throw the door open on his side.

"Now!" I yell at the Duke over the windscream.

His eyes hit me, stunned, he recoils. "What?!"

"Do it!" Stein shouts, swerving the car.

Mike slumps sideways, half way out. Wild cool night wind rushes through his hair. I'm leaned over the seat, trying to hold open the door. Tires whining mad.

"For fucksake!" Stein's gnashing.

The Duke's face is wide open, a terror of racing shadows. He lifts his foot mechanically, weakly kicking at Mike's ass. Mike's reaching back, fumbling, his fingers grabbing loosely at the seat, then sudden gone. Snatched out into dark motion, under the wheels.

We watch, listening hard. Only the hush and rhythm of the road. Sick slow to realize at first but then it begins to repeat quickly. Twenty Mikes are sucked out in rapid succession. A deafening hiss, as if we've stopped moving, the night slammed shut. Maybe it was only a bump in the road. Maybe Mike will drag himself back into the car, faceless and jawless, killing himself laughing.

The Duke reaches across the back seat, pulls the door shut and hangs onto the handle, gagging, swearing at me.

"Okay, go back!" I'm yelling at Stein.

His hands fly around the wheel, fast 180, almost rolling into the gravel ditch.

"Where the fuck is he? Oh, man...headlights."

"I don't see him on the road, they'll go by."

"Where is he?"

"Shut up a minute!"

"There, there! Pull over!"

"Alright," says Stein, hammering the brakes, "hurry up, I'll open the trunk."

Me and the Duke slowly get out of the car, blinking eyeless. We begin to creep across the dark road, watching for Mike to still be moving, talking. But on the other side, at the pavement's edge I make out what seems to be a contented Mike. Just lying around. Almost too small to be him. As if it's a kid in old man's clothing, some strange little creature full of surprises.

We're frozen a few yards away, hunched over, hearing every crackle in the fields. Crickets putting up an impatient chant. The Duke's wavering side to side, peering at the shape on the road.

"Holy shit," he gasps, "his eyes are open!"

"It's okay," I say, grabbing his sleeve, trying to pull him with me. Swear I can see Mike nodding.

"I gonna puke," the Duke groans, tearing away. Goes stumbling down the ditch into some tall bushes.

Stein's back in the driver's seat, his head sticking out the window. "What you guys doing?" he calls.

"C'mere!" I yell hoarse. "We need somethin. Can't just pick him up like this. Stein!"

He hops out of the car, goes around to the trunk and pulls something out. I watch his silouette come toward me. "Alright, keep your balls on. Here, I got the carpet outa the back. We roll him up in it."

Stein looks up, squinting into the deep gray field.

"Where's the Duke going?"

"Fuck him. Gimme a hand."

"A hand," Stein grunts. "What about Mike's hands? His finger prints."

"Yeah, it's weird how he looks okay just lyin here, eh? Only a few bad cuts on his face. No, not too bashed up at all. Looks like he just fell over. Musta broken his neck. Hey, maybe you wanna pull all his teeth out? They could be on record."

Stein lets out a harsh laugh. "What do I look like, a fuckin dentist?"

The Duke comes marching out of the weeds, muttering blindly, walks past us to the car.

Me and Stein flip the small, delicate body onto the carpet and gather up our bundle. I feel the shape inside, slim and rounded. Check over my shoulder for anything left behind. A land crab scurries sideways across the warm asphalt and disappears into the ditch.

⊗

"No problem," Stein grins maniacally, white knuckled on the steering wheel. "we're in the black now. All paid up to Shank and turnin a profit for a change."

"Sure, real winners," I add, taking off my sweat soaked t-shirt. "Let's stop and buy some flowers before we dump him off the spit." I put my leather back on and light a half joint. Take a few long hauls then hand it to Stein. Our faces holding tight, glowing green in the dashboard lights, reflecting good teeth.

Stein drags hard on the joint, turns and yells into the back seat. "Duke! Duke!"

I check up on him. The Duke's passed out. Streaks of puke drying on his shirt front. Burrs on his pants, scrapes on his hands and face from his encounter with nature.

Tires rub on tar so quiet. Stay at the speed limit, put on the seat belt. No stars out tonight. Only a faint moaning coming from the trunk.

Stein catches his breath, we almost look at each other. I reach over and turn on the radio.

17

∞≈

Lacey's cleaning his shades at a stop light on Yonge Street. Thank god he's enough of a fascist to drive a big American car with air conditioning and tinted windows.

We're watching the swarm of shoppers crossing the intersection. Suburban gimps who've come down for the Saturday, searching for the holy stereo deal.

Knots of teenagers are gathered on the south-west corner, clogging the doors to the Eaton's Centre. Semi-literate, north-end mall rats paying respects at their mecca, getting ready to square off and slit each other's throats. Horse mounted cops hover nearby, nervous, tear-gas at the ready.

Lacey puts some classy instrumental on the tape machine as we finally get a green light and pull away south from Dundas Street.

"Man," Lace starts up, "you guys are real patsies, doing Shank's gimmicks..."

"So," I reply, "what's it to you?"

"What's it to me?" he smiles. "I care." His fingertips wipe the corners of that wax mouth. He thoughtfully lights a cigarette with the gold plated butane number and blows out a thin jet of smoke. "You want some good advice, Nick?"

"No, not really."

"I'll give you some good advice," he goes on undeterred. "You oughta stop hangin out with those two losers of yours."

"Oh, yeah? Why's that?"

"I saw you going into one of those fag bistros with the older chick. Very nice, very upscale for a jerk-off like you." He shrugs. "I dunno, maybe you fluked it."

"What would you know about women?"

"I got eyes," he points. "I know style. I know somethin better when I see it."

"Well, thanks for the tip, pops. Maybe I should phone her right now, ask her to marry me. Better still, I'll get a job first."

Lacey's laughing out loud now. Always had this idea to write a *Dear Lace* column. Tell families how it's all done. Instructions in spanking for New Age parents.

"Okay," he says, pulling over to the curb, "here's Queen, get out, the light's gonna change."

"Where you going?" I ask him.

His eyelids sink. "Where'm I going? Get out of the car."

"See yu."

"Yeah, later."

❽

I start heading west, through the shoppers in their pastels, mouths sucking on chocolate covered tumors. All type of American hicks up for the weekend, conventioneers getting harassed by baseball cap, heavy-metal goofs.

Jostle my way past the tail end of a noisy bunch of multi-Toms on parade. Members of the vertical mosaic, yelling off-key through electric bullhorns. Gussied up in a schizoid mixture of jodhpurs, ostrich feathers, pom-poms, animal pelts, spats, tutus, rhinestones, golf caps

90

and multi-coloured tuxedo shirts. A horde of flag waving, psychotically appreciative New Canadians surging over the steps of the Old City Hall. Fierce, tortured smiles stretched across every face, thumb screws turning until they admit to loving this goddamn country.

Looking for cover I work my way across the street full of cabs battling crowded streetcars and duck into the Sherabuck Hotel. Catch my breath in the air-conditioning, come out the south doors onto Richmond Street and hit the liquor store.

Waiting in the line up with a mickey of LCBO scotch, just picking my ass when I turn around and you're right there, behind me. Fuck, I think, the old crow really looks destroyed.

You're smiling shyly, cradling a litre and a half bottle of wine. Jesus, what a sob story. Now what am I supposed to do with you, huh? This is my fault? I had no plans to bother with you again and now you're looking like dogmeat. Naw, listen, I don't have time for this. It's Saturday, y'know.

Coming out of the liquor store she grabs my arm, faking a collapse. I catch her by the wrist. She stares into me limply, like a deaf mute selling sign language cards. Bright daylight, people watching now, eyes on us. What a fuckin drag you are. The dye job's falling apart, gray roots shining tin-foil. I'm pulling her hands off me trying to shove them into her own pockets. Couldn't you at least wear some make-up? Here, gimme the bottle, I'll walk you home. You wanna take a cab? Okay, okay, we'll walk...no, don't start crying...aw, c'mon, gimme a break. I put my arm around her waist, feel the bone. The hip bone's an axhead sticking out of her, scares me. I don't know what it is at first. A wrinkled bag of twigs, going down the pipe in a blue swirl. Her head hanging, hair in her face. I don't believe this. We're moving at a snail's pace up University. A squadron of white stretch limos drive by, honking at a wedding. The bride and groom are arguing in the back seat. We slowly make it up to Queen then west to her place at the bottom of Beverley Street. Each step she's sinking further into the ground and every two-bit consumer with more than five bucks is crowding along this street today. Sick of watching tv, they gotta come down here and get in my way. I'm half dragging, half carrying her now and even the traffic is taking notice. Middle aged couples look on blankly from the car. Kids married, dog died last year, house paid for and retirement set. They'll be killed in a plane crash. Do I need this? I'm hoping nobody I know sees me. You brainless wreck, you're fucking up my life. Finally get to her door. I have to go through her purse for the keys. She sits on the step, rocking, clenching and unclenching her fists. Going through this bag of crap, no money in the wallet, bunches of snot-filled tissue and a plastic vial. Hey, not bad. A dozen or so percodan left from a prescription of 25.

I take her upstairs and get her into the bathtub. She's moaning about her sister and her mother. I light a couple of candles and pour us some scotch. She lies in the water for ages, eyes closed, chanting.

"Alright, enough of this bath. I wanna do some of these percs. Don't want you drowning while I sit out."

"No, leave me alone."

"You basketcase. What do you want me to do, huh?"

Her head slides back, the ends of her hair getting wet. She cups the water in her hands and watches it drain away. "Too bad you're such a coward."

I pull the plug outa the tub and leave her in it. Throw a towel on her. She reaches for me, tugging at my pantleg.

"I'm sorry," she whispers.

"Yeah, I know. We're all sorry."

We end up on the couch with her head in my lap, a ball game on the sports channel and she's faded out good on two percs, as if she needed them.

I do four and keep on the scotch, sink back gradually. The tv is showing sun-drenched bleachers full of shirtless, fat white guys going insane.

I get on the phone. Good party later Kevin tells me. Down on Niagara Street, in the warehouse. The old coffin factory. Lead smelter behind it, slaughterhouse next door, slated for condo brew pub health club conversion. Prime urban lifestyle location. Become a well coiffed John Gacey and it's only steps from your favourite shops.

"Hey, where you been lately?" Kevin's asking.

"On holiday, just got back."

"Yeah, where'd you go?"

"To a dog farm. I might get into breeding them."

"What for?" he howls. "We're already overrun!"

If only it was a joke.

"Listen," he says, "hit the Cameron around midnight."

"Okay, bring what you got. I have somethin to chip in."

"Great, see yu later."

I leave her lying on the sofa, wrapped in the designer terri. Put on the early Iggy tape I made her buy and go take a shower. Use all her high priced hair gunk she's forgotten about. Rifle the drawers for loose cash. Twenty five bucks in the jewellery case, another twelve in a purse in the closet. Sit on the couch next to her for a moment, make sure she hasn't croaked. She's still passed out, snoring like a farmer. I turn off the tv and stereo, pocket the rest of the percodan and leave.

Go west along Queen. Saturday sidewalk jam up. The hippie market's breaking all the sales records. Running stream of chin-tucked hipsters from surrounding hamlets buying up every rusty nail. I'm stopped by one of Shank's ex's, tell her: "Oh yeah, everything's smooth and Shank's okay, yeah, you lookin good, see yu..."

93

Leaves me open to Cassandra come screaming up about the latest guy who slapped her around. She says he's gonna kill me.

"Me?! Why me?!"

"Cuz I told him all about you and he got so jealous and he hit me and ran out saying you were dead."

"What? You ditz!"

I know she wants to put her knuckles to her forehead and faint into my arms but I'm backing up, putting space between us. "I gotta go," I say, "which one is he?"

"The blonde guy, Ronnie. You know, the keyboard player." Cassandra's fluttering those overdone eyelashes, going misty. "He's so angry," she coos. "I was at his house wearing a bikini on the porch and he got so mad. Told me the neighbours don't like it. Then he tells me him and his sister made it and his sister's a lesbian and he thought I should sleep with her too. This guy is really sick and I don't know what I'm doing with him. God, he needs to smoke coke to get it up and hates me when he can't. As if it's my fault. I know what -"

"Shut up a minute. Where's this guy now?"

"How would I know? But he'll be around. He's just so crazy..." She goes all cloudy-eyed and nostalgic. Finally a real paperback romance. Guys bashing each other's heads in over her. Miles of slave armies trying to crash through the gates with battering rams and catapults, boiling oil, the whole bit.

I manage to get away from her and make it over to Stein's house. Him and the Duke are lounging on the back steps off the sunroom. They leer at me coming up the drive, these low smiles on them, sharing a joint.

"Here, take a haul," says Stein, handing it to me, "it's laced. You look like you need it."

That's better, the old form. Shooting the shit, I'm building up this story Cassandra told me. Our balls swelling up about what happens when this musician asshole comes around for me. Decide everything is too good for him. Maybe cut off his prick and sew it up in his mouth. Funny chuffing and one of the roommates calls Stein to the phone. He returns in a few minutes, looking confused. "Arlene got raped last night."

None of us says anything for a while. The Duke lights another joint.

"She was in Western General," Stein tells us, examining the back of his hands. "Now some guys are going out to square things up."

"Who did it?" the Duke asks him.

"It was in Alexandra Park, up near Dundas, behind Scadding Court. That was Jim Arnold. He says it was those greaseballs who hang out there. She was drinkin beer with them."

"Did they really rape her?" I ask.

Stein squats back onto the steps, puts his head in his hands. "I dunno. Jim wanted to know if we're going over to the park with them."

The Duke gives me a sideways frown. "Forget it," he says. "Arlene's got plenty of old beaus who'll wanna mess things up."

"Yeah," I agree, "the cops'll show up and it'll be a stand off. Anyway, we'd probably get the shit kicked out of us."

And nothing happens. Nothing but Arlene blabbing it up, her headphones on, crossing and uncrossing the flayed fishnet legs, smoking all their cigarettes. Nothing but her getting her tongue cut out and an uncircumsized prick somewhere nodding and winking about it.

⇓⇓⇓

Stein turns to the dim comfort of his shoes. Pulls up his sagging socks, ties the shoelaces tighter. The Duke retreats into his festering mouth, feeling the blackened molars. I'm toying with a loose belt rivet, wondering why it hasn't fallen off. An unspoken panic begins to wind through us, a sickening curiosity. We eye each other. Fighting the urge to run up to the park, get down on all fours and sniff the spot where it happened.

18
♈

C'mon, don't get pissed off. I'm just teasin. Why don't you tell me your name?

No, call me Peroxide. That's about your speed.

You get so goddamn straight. Can't even have a laugh.

I know what you're doing. It's a fucking bore.

Don't gimme this. I'm just trying to -

You must be out of your mind. You think you're the only one who has a life? You want me to start calling you leatherhead or something? Wearing all that last year's crap...trying to stud around...fuck...

Look, don't try workin on me.

Why not? Maybe neither of us is so different but we're different from each other. I'm not scared, not that scared, anyway. I'm not lookin for a way in.

You and your neurotic bullshit. You're such a snarky

broad. Every little way you turn is painful. Like you got a bad spine.

Bad spine...sure... I know you really want to be seen with me. There's a thousand guys like you dying to show me off and say, hey, man, here's what my hard-on is worth.

Oh, yeah? You think -

Shut up for a change. Look at this hair, this face, these legs. They weren't made to calm you down. I don't need what you try to do to me. I don't get off on that.

Don't put that on me, you paranoid cunt.

It's not me that's -

You're a vicious fuckin thing. Your ice...

Yeah? You really believe I don't know you?

Know me? What do you know? Holdin back and holdin back, just waiting for this, loving it. Wound up in some PMS nightmare. Turnin everything piss sour.

Oh, sorry I didn't fit the story. I'm really sorry I fucked up your little melodrama. You should've told me and I woulda been a good girl. Frill panties and everything. What you want, huh, baby? Is that how I should do it?

Alright...quit it...shut up.

Look, I fucked you, didn't I? I promised you the moon and the stars and I delivered, didn't I? You think I don't see the way you check me from every angle? Seeing what every shadow does to my skin. I see you wondering how I'll look in five or ten years. Always judging how things will turn out. How much you'll be able to change me. I saw you looking at the price of my hair colour. You and your comparison shopping.

You little fish-hole. I don't need *you* telling me this.

Yeah? Then why did you ask?

I never -

Walked up my steps? Stood there putting me into a black and white frame? Never what? Never would have bothered without the way I look? You ever heard the saying 'fuck yourself'?

19

♥

I'm in the Cameron with Chops, drinking draft. It's early evening, we're waiting for Stein to come back from scoring at the Project. The place is pretty empty, juke box isn't on for a change. Three cowboy-admen huddled over the video game. A couple fossils shuffle in and out of the can.

Arlene walks in. I elbow Chops and we're watching the dead come to life. She sees us, comes over and sits down barely saying anything, orders a Black Horse. Chops goes all humble, only stares into his beer, keeping his eyes off her. She gazes around the room, using us as a prop for not having to sit alone.

Stein comes back, gets defensive when he sees Arlene. Like running across a cripple who's trying to do too much. Wants to smoke her cigarette for her, drink her beer for her, breathe for her. Go home and live every other day in her life for her. Fascinated, we want to make love to a raped woman. Hey, did the cops wanna interview your cunt to make sure it didn't like it?

In the can is written: For A Good Blow Call Arlene.

20

♩♩♩

I run into Shank and his little friend, Peckerhead, up on Bloor Street, in the Annex. They're coming out of one of those rip-off tofu parlours. Shank's fat face folded and mashed in the setting sun. He's faded, badly diluted.

"How's Cheri?" I ask him.

His mouth parts with saliva strings. "Aw...I got rid of her. She was gettin on my nerves."

"Too bad, nice girl."

He grunts, sticks his fists into his pockets. "Okay, I guess, for a hosebag."

Weary and disappointed, totally drained by the tantrum he must have thrown when he beat the shit out of her. A bunch of her clothes and things flying out the front door held in the air by his screaming. The usual act Shank goes through every few months, shedding another skin.

I tell him about Arlene for some reason and he says, "Who?" He's only met her maybe twenty times.

"Oh, yeah, yeah.." he remembers and looks at me like: *So? Yeah? Go on...*

Shank tells me to come along and we start walking east, past the Brunswick House, toward Spadina Avenue, going to his car. Stops in his tracks after a moment, head down and whips out a fold of cash. Peels off a hundred bill, shoves it at the Peckerhead.

"What?" the Peckerhead asks, shrinking back.

"Here," Shank prods, hunched over, this c-note on his fingertips. "Go someplace for a while tonight."

Peckerhead's not sure how to take this. His eyes squirm between me and Shank.

"Don't worry," Shank reassures him, "take it and go. Do whatever you want. I don't need you around right now."

"But -" Peckerhead begs at me, jerking back unsteadily.

"Take it!" yells Shank.

The boy slowly reaches out for the bill. "But I thought..."

Shank finally stuffs the money down Peckerhead's shirt and rushes away. We're marching to the car and don't look back.

"I was wonderin when you'd drop that jack of queens," I tell him.

"Mind your own business."

✛

We tear around town in the Saab for an hour or so going nowhere in particular. Stop in at a few strip joints but Shank doesn't like what he sees so we end up on the top floor of the Eaton's Centre parking lot smoking coke and listening to Boots Randolph tapes.

Shank reaches over to the glove box and pulls out an envelope full of snap shots. He studies each one for an instant then keeps passing over these shots of Cheri. Cock in her mouth, cock up her ass. Summer dress, pretty as a pin in Edwards Gardens. Wearing a fedora in this dumb private-eye pose. Pop bottle up her and with two cute puppies and cooking and in the shower surprised and talking on the phone and holding her own tits and Shank grabs back the photos, looks at them for a few seconds then throws them all over the car parked next to us.

Relaxing against the door, he hangs an arm off the steering wheel and studies me while sucking on his cheek. "So, what are you gonna do?" he asks.

"About what?"

"Drop it," Shank grouses. "You gotta stop sellin yourself short, Nick." He idly runs his hand along the top of the dash, checks his fingers for dust then looks back to me. "You know, I can't figure you out. Still jackin off down on Queen Street ten years after it died. When you gonna get to work, man?"

"You and Lacey," I say. "You sure you two didn't wanna be social workers?"

Big teeth grin. "We are, dickbrain!"

We're both laughing now. Laughing at Shank's stupidity, at the pictures of Cheri scattered over the Ford beside us.

But he's restless tonight so we race up to this disco Shank knows out in Scarborough, start drinking double scotches. He gets into a sports argument with these beefnecks at the other end of the bar and the bouncers have to throw them out. The owner is a close buddy and Shank's giving the guy a hard time.

"Why you let cockscum like that in, eh, Frankie?"

"Hey, Shank," he comes back, "you're in here, aren't yu?"

This is supposed to be funny and cools everybody down. But the goons working the door hate Shank by instinct. Smell his thoughts, smell the ugly thing crawling off his hide tonight. This greasy pig fuck kinda attitude lifting right off him. They smell all about Cheri and the fag and how he's had it up to here and bored and pissed off. They think it stinks of too much money and too much dope and would love to smear his face all over the parking lot. They hate having to wear those red suit jackets and wide ties and they blame it all on Shank. He knows they know and it makes him gleam and gloat at them. They get sick in their nuts and he's glad somebody's hurting about him.

Shank darts a sly face at me and begins talking about his pal who owns this bar. "That's Frank. Frank's a brainless Wop who can't read a matchbook cover. His partner got gunned down in Malton last year, near the airport. But it worked out. Frank got this whole deal to himself, pushed out the widow on the cheap. He's gotta grease the mob and the pigs but it turns over good for him. He's washin out his bread through this joint."

"I don't need to know this," I tell him.

"Why not?" he smiles, throwing a heavy arm around my shoulders. "You should know somethin. The more you know, the more I can count on you, eh, Zorba?"

❋

I drive back down to the city with Shank passed out next to me, seat reclined all the way. His hands keep twitching, thumbs hook into belt loops. The face goes through expressions of doubt, then fear. Cold sweat on the forehead, yellow lights on the Parkway give him this made-up clown look. I'm smoking his Dunhills, put the heater near his hand, burning him. Shank leaps up yelling, fighting for air, eyeballs like dirty dishes. I can hardly keep from laughing.

"Oh, sorry, it was an accident."

He sinks back, sucking on his singed paw, glaring at me as if I'm nuts. Rolls over toward the door and curls up for the trip back to civilization. I've got my face clamped shut, ready to go hysterical. I think of burning his ass. Maybe douse the lights, sideswipe the guard-rail a few times to get his attention. Slam the brakes on at 80 miles an hour, send him hurtling through the windshield.

Watch him catapult out the exploding glass, bounce off the hood and get run over by the screeching tires. Leave his carcass for the night buzzards, raccoons. I'm laughing so hard I can barely drive.

▌▌

We're on the Bloor Street exit ramp behind a line of traffic. Shank wakes up with a start, disoriented.

Far gone, eh, pal? This time it's you. Lost it there for a while. Man, aren't you praising the lord it's me at the wheel?

Shank stares at me, wondering who I am and why I'm driving his car. Pushes the heels of his hands into his eyes, rubbing them, searching for focus. He lights a cigarette, opens the window and inhales the night, glad to have returned. Checking his watch, he turns on the radio. Listens intently as the sports desk rattles off the scores.

"We're two games up," Shank mumbles.

The traffic gets going and we finally make it up the hill to Castle Frank and then down Parliament Street. Shank picks up the car-phone but only gets a high pitched whine so he tells me stop at a Donut Fortress where he makes a few calls.

I wait in the car, watch these two lard-ass cops climbing into their cruiser, loaded down with raised chocolate specials and super extra large coffees. They stare straight ahead, mindless, mouths working through a loaf of shit. Staring right at Shank on the pay phone for nothing else to look at.

He comes bounding out the door, gives them a confident wave. "Evening, gents!"

They keep chewing, expressionless, watch him get into the car.

"Let's go," he says, glancing back at the cops. "What a couple of losers. 37 five a year. Fuckin grunts."

"Where we going?" I ask him, pulling out into traffic.

"I've got a meeting," he replies. "I'll drop you off."

"Okay, front me somethin, will yu?"

"What?" he squawks. "Christ, you're a greedy bastard."

"Hey, I got you back from Scarborough alive, didn't I?"

"Alright, Nick, here's the rest of what I got on me," he cautions, waving the bag in front of my nose. "But, remember, if you lose a step..."

"Sure, no problem." I say, snatching it off him. "You're the king hard-on, Shank."

"Yeah, yeah," he grumbles, sitting back. "I don't know why I bother keepin you around."

21

↓↑↓

I'm loafing around the hippie market, watching Carrot-top throw her sales pitch to browsing mothers and daughters.

"Hi," she squeals at them, "I made these myself. All hand made and hand dyed fabric."

Her dayglo orange hair is kicks for them and ain't it so far out. *Oh, mom, I just have to have this!*

Carrot-top bends over to make change, I'm trying to peek down her shirt, a hick with astro sunglasses on. Another million amp day, sitting on the curb, smoking cheapo, ten buck black tar and keeping an eye out for Cassandra to come around with her siren wailing. Yankee tourists in absurd shorts with ugly kids and beer barrel wives saunter through, staring, mouths open. Useless bags of cornmeal from all-white suburbs of Philly or Detroit. Like Russians with money. They gimme these hostile looks and pull their kids away.

Chops comes back from the bar in the Black Bull, sneaking out with a couple of beers. He hands me one and says, "Dave Sutherland OD'd."

"Who?" I feel like Shank.

"You know," says Chops, "guitar player. English guy, you remember him. Blonde, rockabilly."

"Oh, right. When?"

"Last night. Sat down at a party on Dufferin Street and didn't get up. Nobody noticed him, I guess..."

"Yeah, I guess nobody saw him turning blue."

I tell Carrot-top. She gets really moved and says it's awful how many people been going off the rails lately.

Chops is all droopy about it. "Dave was a good guy," he sighs. "It's a real waste..."

I can't stand it. "Get off it, Chops. You hardly knew him. You think anybody's gonna give a shit when you keel over?"

Carrot-top starts giving me hell. "You're so negative," she yaps. "He had a lot of good friends, y'know."

"Oh, yeah?" I answer. "Like who?"

I'm ruining her sunny afternoon.

"You don't have to be such an asshole, Nick."

"Okay, okay," I'm apologizing. "Relax. Don't get your tits in a knot."

She rolls her eyes at me and asks Chops when the funeral is going to be.

"I heard it's tomorrow," he tells her. "Don't know where, though. The waitress, what's her face, in the Bull. I think she knows."

Carrot-top nods, makes a mental note which must take up half her brain and turns to greet the next eager customer. She quickly clips a pair of brand-name Chinks for a hundred bucks and goes to put the money into her good-karma Indian wallet when this wino staggers up.

"Hey, good buddies!" he blares at us. "What's dis?!"

His fly's undone and his stink, raw sewage. Looking stunned and jovial, as if he's suddenly remembered where all the good times went. Hitches up his rotting pants and pulls off the maimed baseball cap. He grins sheepishly at Carrot-top, a twinkle in his one good eye.

Carrot-top's trying to talk him away. He's reaching out with dried blood hands to get onto her alabaster skin. She

108

throws a desperate look back at me and Chops. Chops leaps to the rescue, starts pushing the guy around. The skid swats him aside and continues courting Carrot-top. He sings to her, bellows out a show tune, arms broad and giving it all he's got.

Be my little lady...

roses are blue and I'm the one...

I stand up but can't bring myself to interfere with his serenade. The broken voice just hanging there for a few moments.

The wino's cracked melody fades with a streetcar clanging it's bell as it goes by. I carefully come up from behind the slob and take him by the arm. He struggles toward Carrot-top, still whispering the feeble song. Chops helps me pull him off the sidewalk and into the parking lot. We lead him over to a wall covered in officially sanctioned graffiti. The wino collapses at the foot of a lime green, cartoon dinosaur drinking a pint of milk. He lies there mumbling, eyes clouding over, hands lightly on his chest. We cram the baseball cap back onto the bald, age speckled head A few people are still monitoring the situation but they're satisfied the problem has been taken care of. Chops goes back to Carrot-top, hoping to cash in on his heroics. I stand by for a minute, looking down at this living testament.

War veteran, has to be, they all are. Wonder if he's gonna die right here behind the tailgate of a brand new Volvo stationwagon. Notice some money spilled out of his pockets, this greasy loose change. I gather it up and put his fist around the coins but he drops them, still trying to speak, to tell his side of the story and how she just led him on. How she's the reason he turned out like this and if only she wasn't such a frozen bitch with a swelled head and she couldn't be happy with any man.

I stuff the change back into his pocket. Want to sit with him, make sure he wakes up but I know these old bastards are tough. Tough it out through an ice age if they have to. Walk to Vancouver for a 26er. If I had a bottle of after shave on me I'd leave it with him. He'd come-to thinking the gods were on his side for once.

Go back over to Carrot-top's stall. She's leaned up against me asking if the skid is okay.

"A minute ago you were hoping the guy would croak," I say. "What's this all of a sudden?"

"I just wanted him to leave me alone," she whines. "I know it's not his fault the way he is."

"Yeah? Who's fault is it then, mine?"

She pulls away, gives me a cross look. "What's wrong with you today?"

"Nothin, my crabs are acting up."

"She's right," Chops pipes in. "You really got somethin up yur ass, Nick."

"Well," I say, showing him my incisors, "nothin you got is big enough, Chops, baby."

"That's gross!" Carrot-top thinks I'm being gross.

"Look," I tell them, "between the two of you you can't even light a match, let alone scare off a wino."

They're about to double team me when the Duke walks up smirking to himself, sussing the deal from half a mile.

"So, Chops," he smarms, "you the junior sales clerk now?"

Carrot-top's had enough, dismisses us with a flip of the wrist and goes back to her wares. "You guys are no fun," she sniffs. Her little Phyllis Diller face and half palsied manner aren't so cute for us no more, we're no fun at all. Just a couple shit eaters left from the floorscum of last night's party. Managed to peel ourselves off the boards and come slithering down the road to make a nice day like this something hot, humid and heavy with carbon monoxide. Exhaling worse than diesel buses without emission controls.

Chops tells the Duke about the guy who OD'd.

"Yeah, I heard," maws the Duke. "Another oil burner conks out somewhere. So what."

I ask him what he got up to last night.

"Oh, brother," he blows at me, winding up for another iron lung story. "Went up to the Fiesta. Dog city. It was like dredging some canal with a barge pole. Pieces of old motor, crankcases covered in eels. All the usual bagged out, over cooked broads. I end up smokin this psycho lamb's bread with that rasta, Nigel, Start walking south on Yonge Street. All the hicks were out in their customized shitboxes. Man, it looked like apes behind the wheel. I got so paranoid. You know, when you wanna start hidin in the bushes."

"Naw, that's crazy," I tell him. "It's the first place apes'll look."

He grins darkly at that and whispers, "art party tonight."

"Yeah, where?"

"A studio on Adelaide, just over here."

Chops is watching us, suspicious, knows he's being cut out again. Still has to try an lever himself in.

"What are you guys doing tonight?" he asks.

"Me and the Duke here," I say, "we're both dating this fat Greek bag I met at a youth dance."

"She digs the double action," adds the Duke. "You know, yu kick out the top legs of the bed and get her on a downslant. It's great, two man bob-sled team."

Chops is enough of a tard to think Carrot-top's gonna be his nurse if he comes down on us. Yelling to be heard by her he says, "You guys are gettin like pimps or somethin!"

"Pimps?" I grin at him. "Sure, we'll pimp any hole you got."

★

111

This art party the Duke heard about turns out to be an album launch media blitz. All the promo hacks dragging themselves out for one more run up the anthill. Real straight arrows continually asking us what we do.

"Nothin, I'm rich. You carryin your condoms? Play it safe, eh, pal..."

There's a wall'o'video showing scratch tapes of Hitler dubbed to a gear grinding soundtrack. Little knots of groover guys standing around, laying it on thick, every last one of them a producer. Sidesliced, two-tone haircuts and baggy, trendwave salesman suits. Always full in the cheek, playing pocket pool with the keys to the BMW. Bragging about how many nightclub line-ups they've stood in. It's like a new year's ball at the Muskrat Lodge. Big hype lift-off for yet another retread mouthpiece and his exciting new release from Passwind Records (Canada) Inc.

"Here, have a complimentary copy."

"No, give it to somebody else. I hate music."

There's synthetic coke making the rounds and we're sticking close to the free bar, listening to these yackity weekend hair-gel chicks going on about Toronto being where it's at.

Whatever you say. Nashville North, Hong Kong West, safe suburb of New York, faggot heaven, idiot's nervana. Toronto *uber alles*. Too bad the weather stinks, eh?

"You guys in a band?" one of them asks.

"Not this again," I crab. "No, I'm not in any fuckin band. You think I wanna be a musician?"

The Duke's rubbing his pants up against one of these big-hair gorrillas, getting off on her black leather mini out of mothballs. I remind him to never try an make a woman who weighs more than he does.

"I know," he answers. "Or has bigger feet."

"Right."

Mine looks like Pierre Burton in drag. She offers me a

tiny zip-seal bag containing about a gram of irradiated pot.

I push it away. "That stuff puts me to sleep. Don't you have any diet pills?"

It's driving them nuts we don't do anything.

"No, no jobs or women or cars or houses or fallen arches or neurotic pets. Nothin. I got the hide on my ass."

↔

I somehow wind up in a rattling Chevette going up Highway 400 at 55 miles an hour with this ugly scar at the wheel. She's jabbering away and I'm staring at her seperated thighs, two sides of beef, each thicker than my waist. Her big tits bob up into her neck every time the car hits a bump and we get to this high-rise in the end of nowhere.

She's all frantic, wad of keys in her hand unlocking half a dozen doors to get into this towering junkpile. I feel weak, used up, this ton sitting on my chest. The scratched out last words of a blind mute cut into the elevator doors. Rayon carpets, macaroni dinner stench in the halls. A door at the end, a number on the door.

She flicks the light on to this one bedroom kitchenette horror story. The swedish furniture, black-dial stereo, bar cart and brass trunk coffee table.

I become separated from myself, watch myself float across the room over to the rust and concrete balcony. A drained ocean out there. Highway lights lead away in green and gold. Stark light empty plaza parking lot with only a cop car lingering around. Probably torturing a black kid in the back seat.

The music she puts on is coming from behind me, another British electro-twirp band. She's changed into this black tent, asking me if I want a drink. Offering the chipped toenail polish and five o'clock shadow shins. The teak dinette set that mother gave or bought or sent.

I'm passing out on the couch, she's getting me undressed. Jesus, who's this hungry, this ambitious? She's got her fingers up my ass - I can't even tell. Pulling me by the ribs. I look down to see if I've got a hard-on. Her dead fish mouth stuck on me, bad breath all over my cock. I wanna boot her in the head. She gives up on the sensual short-course and gets down to squeezing my prick, stuffing it into her snatch like she's trying to hook up a garden hose. I'm slumped across her giant tits between us. Reach down and get a hold of her ass, big enough to show a movie on. We're Laurel and Hardy gone queer. Slapstick wheezing spaghetti sauce show-down out here at the end of the world. I kind of go into neutral lying on top of her, totally out of it. She's working on her clit with me soft, still half inside her. What the hay, she figures, get off anyhow, this guy's going nowhere.

Acts hurt I want to leave two minutes after she gets her rocks off but she's already got the bath running and her robe on. All this see you again soon and phone number and I'll be at the bar this Thursday, yeah, see you soon, bye, you gonna be okay? Oh yeah, I'll take a cab. The music goes off when I'm half way down the hall.

Walking south on Weston Road or Jane Street or who knows. No cars, no cabs. Wide streets, looking like dormant runways, lined with gray apartment towers. Broken only by futuristic gas bars and silent, screaming mall signs. McDeathburgers and Johnny Mufflerface and Factory Wholesale Discount Bargain Outlet.

Dawn begins to rise tired. Slaps the alarm off and cracks open a can of cheap sunshine. Dawn's been out all night like me and she's beat. Doesn't want to bother getting up but, hey, it pays the rent.

A bus rolls by and I catch it back south to the city. The days to come are carefully etched on the face of each passenger. It's early Sunday morning and these church going stiffs all look at me as if I'll be the one digging their graves. They see the dirt under my nails, the flower in my lapel. The driver does not charge me a fare. In their mind's eye they picture me passed out in a nearby field waiting for the drunken priest to get the last rites over with and the blubbering family goes off in the loaded down limo.

Then it's just you and me, my love. I know this day will come. I will fill your hole feeling every handful. Sorting out rocks, pebbles and plastic cups left behind. Taking off my shirt to sweat in the noonday sun, lowering you so slowly, carefully. Backward and backward. I will keep your arms and legs bound with silk, your fingers locked, your chin high and arrange every token thrown into you so you'll know where they are by touch. I will leave the box unlocked for when you decide to walk. Don't be afraid to walk past my house, I won't keep you for my lonely bed. Just walk on to where it was we first met. The streets will not be barren for me. I know what they will say about us, it only feeds me. I don't need to hear that life goes on.

You knew me with long hair falling down. Knew me through the clear girl we both made time for, away from tired role models and disgusted companions. In my arms and in your arms, smooth to the chewed down finger tips. It wasn't the drug that killed you.

22

It's a Wednesday morning, I'm walking Arlene to her counselling. We linger outside the building for a while so she can have a smoke. It's this awkward way between us, bits of words stuck in the throat. The construction across the street is loud, streetcars rumbling past vibrate our feet. I'm thinking about how long I've known her. Since she was fourteen and I was sixteen and how it's something her face hasn't changed much. Just the freckles fading down under her starch dinner complexion. Through the booze and dope and yack she still crashed along, almost too big for her own self.

We're talking about what bands are coming to town and I can't remember ever saying one real thing to her. I'd known her long enough that it didn't matter. Sometimes only hating each other. Mostly hanging around without any effort to be close. The way you see people in your life for years.

I think of asking her what the cops were going to do but she watches my mouth with pursed lips and frosted eyes and makes me hold my tongue.

Her voice got flat, metallic, and she started keeping her arms crossed most of the time. No more goofy walk with mouth full of gum and face jammed into her purse with all this junk jewellery hanging off. No more headphone wires running in the way and hair tangled and big smile, wide eyed, smoking cigarettes by the ton, tripping drunk, funnier than shit. No more nostalgia about those skinny legs and small tits.

I ask her if she wants me to come in with her. She says no. Probably have to wait a while and there's no point, anyway. Try to put my hand on her shoulder, she pulls away without looking at me.

"I'm going in," she says, stepping on her cigarette butt.

"Want me to phone you later?" I ask.

"No, I'll be alright." She turns and walks away.

▶

Head up through Kensington market. Dead chickens swing off the hook, gutted carp lying on store fronts. The stink of Baldwin Street rises to my tongue, tasting the salt blood on the hands of jovial butchers.

Stop by to see this bored slag I know who works in a hep rag shop on Augusta near Nassau Street. The place full of left overs from deadend proms. She gives me some money, sends me out for a mickey and a six pack.

We percolate through 300ml of rye, sick of daylight, listening to the fruit vendor next door call his wife a whore for the tenth time in an hour. Damning the sidewalk merchandise to thieves, she locks the door and turns off the lights. It's all we can do to get through this tangle of underwear and pant legs and bra straps and belts and burn victim siamese twins joined at twilight. On the store floor, fighting to stay hard and stay living. Her tits flipped out over the top of an underwire bra and no lyrics we both know by heart. Making any kind of promise to find the way back, alone. Stars spiralling, laughing openly. Shapes in our water down below, soft underbellies cut like butter. Maybe you ought to get your tubes tied.

23
ᑭᐅᑭᐅ

Me and Stein are at a gallery opening in the ARC 'space', trying to carp some free beers. In amongst art scene weeps loitering like it's a church basement mixer, putting mineral water in their wine and smoking superlights. All this touchy-feely anti-flesh art stuck to the walls in wet strings and miles of text explaining why this is gonna get you to take a good whiff of yourself.

About to leave when I see the petrified battle-ax herself. She looks at me vaguely. Maybe I was the guy at the bus stop this morning. Or maybe I was the guy hanging in her closet or the thing lurking under her bed, the rapist plumber or even the pedophile postman who took away the daughter she never had. Yeah, it's me, sweetheart. How about one more time around the carousel?

She's with another man. Oh my god, *another* man. Older than her for a change, going gray, going bald. Where'd you leave your hair, mister? With the first wife? Boy, she really cleaned you out, eh?

I'm tempted to make a scene, freak out on the guy, on her. Force her to tell him what was between us. But I'm sure she already has. During their long walks in leafy parks, discussing her problem, her past, her options. He'll nod seriously, compassionate type. Stops right on cue, takes her by the elbows and gazes into her eyes for a long and special moment. He's a man, it's no lie. Not a spindly armed vicious bastard with the soul of a tube worm. No, a man, with convictions and emotionally complex to be sure.

They begin to walk again. His arm protectively around her shoulders, she rests her head on him. Don't worry, he tells her, we're all going to help you. I'll do what I can and you know your family really loves you. You're not alone in this, we understand it's a sickness and has to be dealt with like one. One step at a time. You have to wake up everyday believing that --

Yeah, yeah, shut up already. I know what she wants better than she does because I know what I want. And I look at her and it's clear as a fucking bell she's dying inside out, side to side and from the core. You, you bald, middle-aged excuse for a dog's ass, you're not even dead. Just this tweed and elbow patch joke, a camouflaged slug.

Stein notices my fuming, trying to smoke a whole cigarette in a single drag. He's looking at me as if I just barfed all over myself. "What's with you, Nick?"

"Her," I say, still staring across the room.

"Oh," he figures out, glancing over. "So, what about her? You still hung up on her? Man, you're crazy. She mighta been okay for a while, but she's two years away from the bedpan. You know, you're really sick."

"Why? Cuz she's older than me?"

"Older? She looks like Vincent Price with a hang over."

I start laughing. Stein breaks into a grin, can't keep a straight face.

"Stein," I tell him. "I think I'm really shook up."

"You're always shook up. You're fucking insane. Why doncha go over and say hello to her? Be a human being for Christsake."

"What? Talk to her?"

"Yeah, with your big mouth. You remember how to use it?"

"Hi, how yu been?"

She's startled for a moment, her lips in a silent O.

"Hi, I'm...uh...fine, fine..." She turns and gestures awkwardly to her new man. "This is my friend, Ted. He writes for tv."

"Hello, how are you?" says Ted, giving me the dead fish handshake.

"Awright..."

She's treading on hot coals, smiling like a rookie stripper. Ted's rocking on his heels, his eyes scan the crowd as if he might know a lot of people here. Yeah, sure. I feel like kneeing him in the nuts.

"So," I say, noticing her chest bones sticking out, "you lost a little weight, eh?"

"Oh. Well. I've been -"

"Look, *we* don't want you here!" Ted shouts, suddenly boiling over.

"*We?* Who's *we*, flathead?!"

"We as in not *you!*"

"Don't point at me, you old bag of shit. I'll kick yur fuckin ass!"

The prattling crowd of art pukes around us begin hubbubbing.

"Just leave us alone!" Ted yells.

"Piss off, man! You got her ownership on yu?!"

She's panicking, pulling at him, gibbering at me, eyes going feverish. People start crowding us, all these hands reaching out saying *calm down, calm down*. I let some earth shoe have my elbow in the mouth. Ted puts his hand out toward me. I catch him in the throat with a wild

120

roundhouse. He gags for a moment, then rushes me. I'm diving out of his way, kicking at him. He's half spinning, punches me in the chest as he falls, bowling over some of the crowd. Stein's arm gets me around the neck, dragging me out.

They don't bother coming after us. Stein shoves me down the sidewalk and looks back to be sure. "Shit!" he yells, wacking at the side of my head. "Can't you relax for once?!"

We're walking east along Queen toward Bathurst, late sun afternoon dead, no dimensions. I'm telling the panhandlers to go light and even snarl at Rosie, the dwarf whore. I stop, turn to Stein. "Let's cook at yur place."

"Take it easy," he says, getting sick of me, "it's still early."

"C'mon, my nerves are shot!"

"Shut up. We'll smoke a joint, have a beer. We gotta save the satin for later, moron! What the fuck is wrong with you?"

"Nothin," and I start walking again.

Slide down the sewer into the Cameron. Arlene's sitting by herself next to the jukebox. Great, she's all I need. Her head comes mechanically around toward us. She's too spaced out to notice my sweats but Stein gestures at me and tells her: "Studley here freaked out over some ex at this gallery shtick we crashed."

Arlene nods once, barely, and murmurs something. I wanna smack her in the face but I just take one of her smokes, snap off the filter and light it.

*

Rough skin I uncovered pulling off black leotards at her from behind with the skirt still on, using it as a harness. Wild mane of star burned hair and on my knees, expert rider. Push, balls sucked right in, held tight by

121

internal night vision organs. Side view of her canal, entry way, gliding through to the hotspot. She's on all fours, looking down between her swaying tits, face red, catching her breath in time with our gallop. I'm stuck to her, giving her back those cloud shaped purple bruises on the ass, slow cut lacerations never explained away. Calculated to enrage the other side because she won't complain, won't condemn. Okay, convince her to have a future then, force her to believe a baby would make the difference. But you'll have to kill her to get my seed out. It hides in her, a time bomb. Going off when the days again begin to seem only like days and the evenings just pass. Getting home to an empty house, hearing the kids playing in the street outside. Asking why and phoning her work but already knowing she hasn't been there and sensing very well where she is. Having a heartless heart attack, only then remembering her sleepy words about how pretty, how desirable I can be. And he is suddenly plunged by all there is to own. His prized reclamation project and I have disappeared on first class passage to exotic skinned lands. Grief for you, Ted, my brother, sincere grief, telling yourself you're only human after all and noticing that secretary at work for the first time perhaps. Really seeing her, though she's a little reticent, reminds you of your runaway and how that had begun. Studying this secretary as she functions behind the flourescent bathed desk, you're pondering something friendly, casual: dinner and hotel. With one single hard-on guarded and psyched up all day long. Clean socks and planning every detail. Well, you console yourself, when my runaway comes home this won't matter. It's harmless, an adult circumstance. But then getting sick excited, feeling risqué, you finally have her in your car, the new American job with a stupid name. She agrees to let you make a deposit as her glowing pink nails graze the vinylette seat cover. Her mouth is shut though your ears are howling. News comes on the radio, reporting you and a universe like you. But it's a piss off that this secretary or accounts payable comptroller or whatever the fuck she is, it pisses you off she's speechless, her pert little blonde head only staring out at the street full of parapalegics walking, abusing you at stop lights. Hideous comics moving against the colours, laughing at your sporty model. How can they be so much lighter than air? The laughter of fully charged skies.

At a reserved table in a monkey suit restaurant, talking about what you both read in the paper today. Offended by second hand smoke on a dying planet, deeply concerned about the third world and you see my face in your plate. With aching balls and a fat ass you feel us somewhere, my teeth in the neck of the woman you so painstakingly reorganized. And you know why I do it. Don't love her, don't save her, make her a demilitarized zone and I'll stay clear.

In your fax equipped hotel room finally. Once in the bed with curtains drawn. Soundless rhythm with your face in the pillow next to the secretary's ear saying how good how good. Good god, look at the time. You drop the condom into the toilet and watch your drowning sperm spin away. Washing your dick in the sink, toilet paper wipes off her dry cut. Telling yourself to get rid of this one because she knows everything and was on the expense account, anyway. Telling yourself it is not true that your rationalized heart throb is with me right now, getting stoned on your money. Telling yourself to be ashamed at getting a hard-on thinking of us stuck together, guts locked. Recalling how she stood on the balcony, so lovely, waiting for the foul summer garbage wind to bring me back. Forgetting you completely the instant you're out of sight.

▲

I'm brewing in this elaborate revenge, watching the midget waiter putter around the bar. Stein's reading the weekly throw-away, pointing out something in the personals column to Arlene. She responds so meekly, out of breath. Always letting her cigarette ash gather now.

Listen, it's not your nice guy man I hate. It's the lack of possibilities. I woke up stoned the morning after you left for the last time, still tasting your lipstick, wondering where you went and you know how much I hate sex. It took everything I had to keep myself from chasing after you. It murdered me to think of how you'd rush down bringing coffees and cakes and cigarettes and money and books you knew I would never read. Your passive ways leaving me no choice but to deny you until I was alone and couldn't believe I really was not The One. Left only to crave the salt sea smell of you, plowing this crease between my eyes when I should be plowing the rut between your legs. Going through tough jungle air, hardly breathing, to where your cervix lives on an altar. Put you up on every used pedestal made of gold and diamonds and marble and rare opals and moon rock and built with mythic skill. Make you wild and unreachable, as every man full of terror and bad genes does.

I pace my floors and can't stay alone, can't be in the same room where I remember you asking. Dressing the way you always liked to see me and driving myself out into the street to push aside the admission that there was nothing to touch and nothing to hold. Not even a shadow left behind. Just our sickening vocabulary of intimate affections. Words made absurd by us repeating them so often. Slow, lobotomized kisses we will both be embarassed to remember. Knowing I won't recognize your voice, the difference of your hands. Shit-mouthing you to anyone who'll listen but then reminded of you when the phone rings and I've got to guess who's coming on so familiar and I'm faking it along without a clue, forcing myself to laugh out loud and tell the sound of love I've gotten over that sort of thing.

We did nothing but kill time waiting for the next chance to kill time, a mangy excuse to be *involved*. Never losing the ability to think straight. Maybe you ought to make a decision to be with that caring, older guy. Forge a strong relationship, fulfill his sublime little desires stuck sideways into a constipated upbringing. The two of you held tight with joint accounts and lengths of rusted wire running through the guts.

Anyway, you never could pronounce my last name properly, even with your fucking correct soda-cracker Anglo grammar. Well, this is *my* language now.

Yeah, I know. I have no right to hold anything against you. Our blood was only warm on the road, living off friction. Skin on skin, we took a ride of bad debts and bad gas mileage. Past sleeping Ontario villages next to the 401. Cursing the dreams of slumbering rednecks who would have us lynched in daylight. Drawing closer than death, than wombs that need filling. For a brief moment even the sun falling behind us on the highway and the moon going north to south couldn't keep up, the stars on the horizon blinking good-byes. Through flatlands and badlands and mountains getting smaller we fled. Without families, without failures, without our father's names.

24

◆

I never spoke to her again. Once, while sitting at the Rivoli patio I saw her walk by. She didn't notice me and I kept from saying anything. She looked alright, except her clothes were straighter. The Duke and Arlene were with me. He arched his eyebrows and Arlene, who by that time had entombed her past said "what? what?" while looking around.

"Nothin," I told her. "A jalopy I used to own just went by."

I'd heard she'd moved out of the neighbourhood and she was never in the bars anymore. I wondered if she was still being renovated by Ted, the tenured culturcrat, if he'd suckled her back to health. Yeah, of course, the great Canadian recuperation. The expert animal handler, he'd conned her with favours, perks and full coverage benefits back to the land of the concerned.

Hey, maybe we can just be friends.

Okay, we bombed at the box office, never got off the ground, so what. Everyone's clued in to production values now, no more free ride gags. Even Shank is keeping in step with the times, flogging his watered down coke-lite to those who have to get up in the morning, strap on a four-cylinder hemorrhoid and spend the day breathing recirculated gases. Gagging on the news, another random attack of doubt, another opinion poll brutally murdered. Ample evidence that what goes around comes around. The full moon day when pets eye their masters in mistrust and you realize you'll have to have children to prove you were ever here.

The same day Shank was entertaining our crew and had a sudden seizure. Howling rabid as usual one minute then on the floor twitching. We stood there looking down at him going blue, clawing at his chest, and waited for him to die. Crouching next to him, seeing his tongue curl, teeth trying to crawl out of his mouth, I throw a glass of water in his face but nothing doing.

So we load him into the Saab and cruise over to the hospital. I'm driving casually through traffic, the Duke on the passenger side, arm lazy out the window. Stein dozing in the back with Shank gacking, gurgling, eyes turned up white.

Pulling into the emergency ramp, we get out and walk away, leaving him there, the car still running. Glancing over my shoulder as we move up Bathurst Street away from the hospital, I see a few orderlies yelling, dragging Shank out of the car. No, Shank couldn't die, not yet. His hands were full of lines. Any fortune teller could reassure him. Three days later we dropped by to see if he'd had the baby.

"Hey, Shankorama," I greet him as we stroll in, "did they sew the tits on you yet?" It's real sweet seeing him like this. Weak, a tiny fart full of tubes.

"You bastards," he grimmaces theatrically, "leavin me to die. You think I couldn't tell what was going on?"

"We took real good care of you, Boss," warns Stein. "You oughta remember that."

"Fuck..." Shank shifts painfully. "I should get Lacey to off you pricks. You're lucky you're not worth the price."

"What a tool," says the Duke, deeply disappointed.

"Doesn't even know his buds."

Shank's layed out in a private room, propped up with a minature tv in his face. Surrounded by stainless steel shit troughs and piss bottles. Bags of fluid hooked up to his arm, bleeping machines soothing his fear. A lot of high priced, hi-tech, electronic junk keeping this maggot alive. His little wristband name-tag on, the dying mafia boss, just another patron with high blood pressure.

"Listen, Shank," I say to him, "we wanna score. You're no good to us like this."

"So? Go hit on niggers up in the Corridor for a change. Or how about the chinks? Those gooks are taking over this country, anyhow. You better get friendly with them."

"Get real," says the Duke. "We wanna do a bit of a front."

"Yu don't say?" replies Shank, getting martyrous. "Well, you're gonna have to wait then."

"So tell me," Stein steps in, fingering one of Shank's cables, "what's *this* tube for?"

"Quit fuckin around!" Shank yells. "Leave that alone!"

"What the hell," carps the Duke, "maybe we can jump start him."

"C'mon, Shank," I'm bugging him. "You're the monster who's always going on about keeping straight. We been right on the line for you, man."

"Okay, okay..." he resigns, turning away from us. "Get a hold of Lacey, he'll do it. I'll call him."

Stein pats his shoulder. "That's real white of you, Shank."

Shank pulls the tv down in front of his face, can't bear to look at us. "You guys..." he grumbles. "Can't gimme a little peace. It's always me that's gotta look after yuz."

As we're leaving I bend over, kiss him on the ear and whisper, "thanks a lot, mom."

≡ ≡

Lacey does the proxy deal with the formality of a foreign exchange banker. His hands staying clean of origins, sleeps with a clear conscience. He fronts us precisely six-tenths of a gram of beige. Makes a coded note calculating our current equity and disposable income.

But to Lacey we're only one of Shank's costly eccentricities, a red ink disaster, derelict billboards advertising products you can't get parts for anymore. Cracked pieces of obsolete V-8 motors sticking up through tall grass in the untended backyards of Parkdale homes long hacked up into shoebox bachelorettes. Back alley tin gates that haven't been opened since Bill Dennison was mayor. Sucking on take-out coffees, the lid chewed through. Feeding on pizza slices and breakfast specials, beans on toast and canned left-overs. Entertained by bankrupted businesses, foreclosed mortgages and cars towed away by the cops. Sleazing through the bar, oily hands reaching for a fresh peach, trying to see her legs.

"You never been here before? It's okay, used to be a lot better."

25

I'm waiting at the light to cross Spadina. Stein's beside me, scraping something off the bottom of his shoe, complaining his feet hurt.

"Sure they do," I say, "those things are two sizes too small."

"They'll stretch."

"Yeah, everything does."

Stein nudges me and points across the street, past the billowing noonday traffic.

"Don't point, you asshole."

I can see that peroxide mop through the stream of cars, she's already out in the first lane. White legs impenetrable to any sun. This confiscated look about her. Feel as if I'm watching her through a key hole.

The lights change and we start crossing. I'm grinning dumb as she glances at us for a second and says hi. We both say hi and turn, walking backwards for a few steps, watch her rushing away.

"Can't even be civilized," I complain.

"Waddya want?" Stein harps at me. "You got it on with her for a while, right? You expect every lame-assed hairbag to drop everythin for you? I tell you, Nick, you're a real headcase."

"You a feminist now, Stein?"

"Sure," he replies, pulling out the old gag. "Maybe I'm a lesbian. I like girls too."

We shuffle along Queen Street past the Horseshit Tavern. The CBC is shooting some made-for-tv malakia on the sidewalk in front of Edward's Books. Another insomnia cure slice of CanCon with the usual collection of motor homes and moving vans. We're edging around, hassling these serious film types with their electrician belts and walkie-talkies. Linger near the equipment trucks, sniffing for something to rip-off. Watch the crew perform their high pressure act for the passersby. We're babbling at them about wasting taxpayers money.

"Hey, how much you make, anyway?"

This assistant ass-kisser wearing a million-pocket location vest comes over and gives us the *hey guys* line. I guess we're too stupid to figure out they're good for the local economy.

Stein's right on this dolt's case. "You need an operation, buddy. You walk like a fag."

"Watch it!" he points at us, laying on the heavy glare.

"Yeah, I was," replies Stein, "that's why I'm tellin you. Better do somethin before you wake up with a hard-on stuck up your ass."

The CBC clone is getting steamed, about to blow his government payroll cool.

"Aw, take it easy on the guy," I deadpan. "He's just practicing his craft."

The rented cop comes over to shoo us away. This semi-conscious Scotsfart who doesn't want to be out in the sun.

"Do me a favour," he says, looking dead beat. "Get lost."

"Yeah, okay," I'm chuckling, "we're only givin these hingeheads a hard time."

"I know," answers the cop, looking back at the crew, "they're real parasites, but c'mon..."

131

We get on our way, strut through giving the finger, asking the wardrobe women if they wanna come for a stick shift ride. Veering onto the road to avoid the sidewalk hippie market we head for the pizza slice joint at Beverley Street. Run into Chops and Cassandra coming from her room above the Black Bull. Stein's in a gregarious mood, confronts them right off.

"Hey, you two gonna raise chinchillas together?"

"Chops bought me this necklace!" Cassandra shrieks, pulling down her black stretch polyester almost to the nipples. "Nice, isn't it?"

A plastic bauble from the hippie market.

"Aw, Chops," I mush, "you're a real honey."

He makes a face at me. "Yeah, I am. We gotta go, see youz later."

They hurry off with Cassandra fixated on the prize hanging between her tits. Chops stops about ten feet away, comes back.

"I know about Cabbagetown Mike," he hisses at us.

"Know what?" I move closer.

"I just know."

Stein grabs a handful of his shirt. "You'd better know fuck all, Chops."

We both bear down on him, right in his face. Chops' thin, pale mouth hangs tough. "I just know," he repeats.

Cassandra's looking back at the three of us. "What are you guys doing?" she yells.

Chops takes a quick look at her, turns again to us. "Don't worry," he grinds, breaking free. "I'm not sayin nothin."

Me and Stein look at each other, I gaze back at them disappearing up the street.

"What's he on about?" I mumble.

Stein says nothing for a moment, wipes his forehead on his sleeve then eyes me carefully. "Been talkin in your sleep, Nick?"

132

26
×××

Shank got out of the hospital eventually and I went up to see him. It was all clean slates and clear sailing from here on in.

"You don't live forever," he tells me, squeezing a lime into a glass of ice.

"Well, thank Christ for that," I say.

"What do you know?" he scoffs. "I was almost there, man. I realized a few things. I'm gonna take care of myself and fuck everybody else."

"New leaf, eh?"

"You got it. No more of these loony broads. No more blow out partying. No more weirdos hangin around."

"Sure," I agree, "you're not a young man anymore."

He gives me a fed up look while pouring mineral water into the glass.

"Hey," I nod, "the good stuff."

"You wanna kill yourself, go ahead," says Shank, lifting the glass to his lips. "I'm not going out the side door like so many of these wipe-outs. You're just waitin for the big one. You and those two door knobs you hang out with."

"What was it, anyway?" I ask him.

"A heart attack," he replies, patting his chest. "Waddya think? Too much stress they told me. Gotta get outa the pressure cooker."

"Yeah, the pressure cooker," I echo. "Maybe you oughta get into gardening. Put on the sunhat, some grape juice, classical music all the time...maybe move out to —"

"Shut up, Nick."

"Alright, alright...Listen, Chops says he knows about Mike."

"Chops," Shank grunts. "What's he know?"

"Nothin. But why would he say that?"

"You're too paranoid. He's only tryin to get on your nerves."

"Yeah, well, it worked."

"Forget it, not worth it. Anyway, I got somethin else for you to do."

I can feel the scum rising. "Yeah?"

"Yeah, have a peek at what Cheri's up to these days. See who's workin her."

"What?! You just said no more crazy broads!"

"Yeah, yeah," Shank dismisses me. "You'll take my camera. I wanna see how she's lookin now."

"It wasn't that long ago."

"Just do it. But don't let her see you. C'mon, I'll rent you a car. She knows mine."

∠∠∠

So I'm sitting around in this rented econocart, listening to a hep DJ tell me what a gorgeous day it is. Feel like a pervert waiting for Shank's former irreplaceable to come out of a townhouse complex near Steeles Avenue and Don Mills. Out here at the metro limits with the gnomes and wartpickers.

It's close to an hour before Cheri walks out wearing an all white, skin tight body suit. Thin gold belt and matching high-heeled sandals, designer dance bag and these big sunglasses. I don't make an effort to hide, she

134

sees me almost right away. Stops, lowers her shades and stomps over.

"He sent you, didn't he?"

"Yeah," I reply, turning down the radio.

"Well, what is it?" She's ready to spit tacks at me.

"Nothin. I'm supposed to see how you're doing. Shank didn't want you to know."

"What? Is this a joke?"

"No, he wanted to see how you look now," I tell her, holding up the camera. "You know, see if you're alright."

"Is that so?" she asks, burning at the edges. Cheri narrows her eyes at me, looks at the camera for a moment and then storms off, disappearing between the parked cars. In a few minutes I see her pull up the driveway to leave and snap a quick shot of her hunched over at the wheel.

27

Chops had been avoiding us, was spending a lot of time with a young art poodle. One of the baby-hippie crowd, friendly bunch of kids who'll tell you war is bad and peace is good.

I find him sitting alone in the Cameron during the afternoon. Dark and cool, echoing airplane hangar. A few rounders and their apprentices drinking draft for day time prices.

"Heard you been workin the art college cafeteria," I tell him, taking a seat.

Chops isn't saying much, keeps his eyes to himself.

"I'm not going away," I say. "I don't give a shit what you do. Just watch your mouth."

His face fixes on me. "I'm not talking about you."

"Yeah? You're a righteous little prick."

"I'm not sayin anything to anybody. I don't care about that."

"What then?"

"It's just that -- I seen Mike out with you guys a couple weeks ago. I heard he crossed Shank. It doesn't take much to figure -- Listen, I only want you to know that I know," Chops says softly. "That's it, Nick."

"That's it, huh?"

"Yeah..." and he looks down into his lap.

I take one of his smokes and get up to leave. Walking out I pause at the door, wondering why I gotta know worthless shits like him. All wanting deep down inside to do the right thing. Me getting fucked up about a guy I wouldn't wipe my ass on. Made me sick I'd worry about his effect. Stuck with having to balance my end in the face of impossible odds. The lord and everything else piled up on the other side of the chain.

It's the middle of the day outside, hot as the devil's ass. Air conditioners blowing a chorus. Nobody shops, nobody walks. Deadsville. I stagger toward Stein's, swearing to myself about that moron, Chops. Fighting for every scrap of shade along the way. Stop in at Danny's Pool Hall, drain a few cans of pop and listen to another one of his landowner harangues.

On scorching days like this the place smells of Danny's dead dog. The way he nursed that suffering thing. It's bones gone rubbery, spine twisted into a corkscrew. Danny would go down into the basement with a plate of mashed up noodles in warm milk and practically breast feed the bitch. The 80 year-old ex-miner who was going to outlive us all. Smiling grimly to himself whenever cheque book groovers would come around, their eyes measuring his pool hall and his coffin for future retail perversion. Danny with two fingers left behind in a North Bay strip mine and still selling cigarettes at 1965 prices. Pulling out the old coffee stained atlas to point out his birthplace on a forgotten eastern European border. He'd sit in the window and wave every time I went by. Even if I didn't wave back, no matter, next time. Yeah, next time I promise to stay a little longer, Danny. Show a real interest and learn how to shoot straight on the big table.

Danny coughing hard, spitting up some dark stuff into a piece of newspaper. Carefully sifting through it with a pencil to make sure he wasn't coming apart at the seams like Stein who's lying in his dank, tacked on room. Sprawled out as if taken down with a .12 gauge shotgun. Flopped out on the cat clawed mattress with his mouth dragged open, a shoe losing its sole. His fitful slumber amid scribbled reams of illegible genius.

I sit in a chair at the foot of his bed and consider this 32 year-old semi-corpse. Wheezing and groaning, always one step from death's doormat. Completely wiped out from the hairshirts and self-mutilation, the pennance and begging for forgiveness. I want to wake Stein up, force him to his feet, make him come out into the liquid hot sun. Tripping blindly, hands reaching out, caneless.

Stein finally opens his eyes around dusk and isn't surprised to see me. Tells me what a good sleep he had and asks if I've got anything.

I pull out a joint. He lights a cigarette and smells his feet, sticks a hand down his pants and peels his balls off his thigh. Takes the joint and drags deeply, the smell of burning plastic.

"I had the weirdest dream," he tells me.

"Yeah, what?"

"You were in it?"

I take it a little hard. "So, it's my fault?"

"No, no...you were selling tickets to people getting on a train but then not letting them on."

I'm skeptical. "What?"

"You had this accent," he says with a messianic gleam in his eyes. "Like a spic maybe."

His mind drifts off, I take back the joint.

"A spic," I mutter, "fuck you."

"Relax," Stein yawns, stretching, "it was only a dream."

"You dream like an asshole."

"Yur nuts..."

"Oh, yeah? You think dreams are a joke?"

138

"Man..." Stein groans, "you're such a downer. You gotta start thinkin positive. It's the only way you'll ever get on top."

The Duke arrives, catching the end of Stein's pep-talk. "On top?" he asks, walking in. "Who's on top?"

"*We* are," Stein answers, leaning back, pleased with himself. "Just follow me, boys."

And as the evening gets lighter we become darker, almost to evaporate. Find the higher order Stein's on about, think big for a change. Declare ourselves to be the International Miscreant Fund, appeasing the rich with tax breaks on suppositories. Determined to lead the heroic struggle back to lower costs and higher productivity. Reverse the polarities on this clean-freak burgh, make it give up something of muscle and bone, demand a profile on the inside track. Whine and bitch that everybody needs somebody sometime. The sweet-fingered advocates, bringing on heavy-hype coverage and indepth analysis, careful not be left on the scrap pile of last year's oil spills, unsolved murders and worthless quotes. Develop a real zeal, a shark attack lust for staying in the middle of the eye, a greasy thumbprint on the news-pulse lens. Mobbed by every kind of electronic retrieval and storage device, papparazzi and pop stars at our heels, instamatics and full sized crews. Tanning under blazing video lights, clusters of microphones demanding to know the latest score. Shrewdly leased out to every talk show and as standard equipment in all safe sex devices. Shoppers dive at our feet, pleading for forgiveness. We're swarmed with handlers, coordinators, managers, AIDS-negative groupies. Finally get off the hook by signing a deal for the movie of the poster of the book.

"Don't worry," we're told, "you'll be a hit in this town, everything is."

This is the spread-sheet vindication. To walk with heads held high, roll on up Spadina Avenue to The Crest

Grill and take the holy communion of coffee boiled by the mighty hand of the sceptre wielding proprietress, Mister Helen. Look on soberly as she gives a fast-talking infidel the bum's rush. We assume our stations at the counter, joining the men of noble girth and observe their discourse on the day's races at Greenwood.

Old Sam, one the rock-hard regulars, holds his corner table, sipping black coffee from a take out cup and carefully combing over his bald spot. His baleful, watery eyes light up at our arrival as he greets us equally and begins complaining about the distance to his new welfare housing.

They cleared off this corner at Spadina and College Street. With handcarts and handouts, bribes and beatings. Only two or three of these vericose faced dinosaurs are left between the cracks. Cut off their water and tobacco and they'll soon fade out, a scratchy record slowing down.

We're asking Sam who'll be filling in when they're gone.

"Forget it, fellas," Sam advises, while rolling himself cigarette. "they've cleaned up this town. Naw, you don't wanna do this. Hangin around ain't what it used to be. Go on down the block to the car wash, maybe some work there. Or ask Gwartzman if he needs any casual help. You know he gives a square deal when he can. Yeah, I had a little work at the United Dairies but they moved uptown, eh... After Shopsy's left the neighbourhood, things have never been the same... I heard this textile place, down here near Oxford Street -- You know it? Yeah, I heard he takes on day labour once in a while, pays cash too. And the live chicken company further along, they might be able to use some handlers.

You ever drive cab? Yeah? Me too, years ago. Now there's a lot of amateurs in the business... I was thinkin of night school but I'm gettin too old, no point really, got my pension coming next year... Don't like the room they gave me. The city, they gave me this place way out near Etobicoke. It's clean an all but too far. Nothin doin out there, eh. I used to have a room over here on Bathurst, just north of King Eddy Public School. Nice old couple had the house. Mr. and Mrs. Paster, nice people. But they both passed away a few years and their kids sold the place. I couldn't afford the new rent so I moved into the Waverly Rooms, cost me a fortune. But the city came through about a month back. Guess I was lucky...You boys been to the track lately? No? Me neither. Been there only twice this summer. Was on a bad streak and things didn't improve. Figure to lay off it till fall. Never much luck in this weather. It's the humidity, gets to the brain, can't think straight. Actin crazy, pickin longshot triactors... Headin off, boys? Okay, see yu around, eh?"

Yeah, Sam, we'll see you in the line up onto the boat. Keep a silver dollar for the captain and don't worry if he gives you any trouble, it's a lot of bluff. He might call you this or that and try to make fun of you in front of everybody -- keep your cool. If you've got the coin he'll let you come across. He's a greedy drunk and never takes a holiday. But you'll be alright. The captain likes the old boys, the worn at the heels crowd who's hands are almost never out of their pockets. We'll bring along a bottle and convince you to start drinking again, at least for the occasion. Come stumbling down the embankment arm in arm, singing and shouting dirty limmericks.

So we'll go no more a roving so late into the night...
Fall into a messy single file like the old days at the labour pool. One upping each other with famous cock stories. Slapping backs and bumming smokes. Trading rumours on rooming houses and where to get drunk for cheap on Sundays. All together and in the clear. Naked, drooping assless, fumbling with stringy underwear. Scars on the bone, swollen joints and tattoos gone green and

141

shapeless. Appreciating the hot water and clean towels at the Harrison Baths. Saving the longer butts behind the ear.

Grab your accordion, Sam. I've got the tape machine, the Duke's on bullhorn and Stein's strapping some tin cans to his chest. We'll fire up the old diesel powered heartaches and hoof it down Spadina to the market. Twirling tire irons like batons. Zigzagging through, picking up voodoo dancers and jobless skinheads along the way, paying the ransom on sweatshop slaves. Taking the last big chance.

28
●▼●

Squeeze into the Cameron Pub as they're shouting last call. Herpy, the barhand, is telling everyone to get home and get to sleep. It's a week night, y'know.

The crowd suddenly has the guts cut out of them, a thin murmur about what could have been, what should have been, what might have been.

Yeah, yeah, I don't make the law. I'm just tryin to make a buck. C'mon, get out.

Θ

I run into the woman I should have married about three centuries ago. Ravishing as usual, more scrupulous than ever. She sees all the expressions I've worn since the day we met. Her cherried lips are sympathetic. She offers her hand: small, soft and lethal. I know she could unbuckle me with one word. Try to guide the conversation back to her and her life. How we shouldn't have seduced each other's friends and should have believed everything we told one another. In her I can see her mother and her mother's mother reminding her how far she can go. Those two bearded hags always hung on the periphery, never letting her decide in a vacuum. Never let her be dragged off by her own cunt and be thrown up when the night puked and groaned at first light. Kept her safely outa my reach but she'd secretly wait on the phone, accepting tokens of affection, weighing them against the long term.

Anyway, momma's little girl, buy me a shot before they close down this dump, will yu? I'm dead broke and I wanna spend some of your daddy's money.

Tiny purse snaps open to a new set of twenties. Change in a separate compartment and proper ID. Well, I'm glad at least you managed to become someone. Yes, sugar, I know some of those duds in the back of the bar and yes, they still consider this a fine night out. No, I haven't seen so and so lately... Say, how's your mother, anyhow? Naw...don't give me an elaborate tale. I was only being polite. How about your mute brother, still hung up on old skin? I'd like to compare notes with him sometime... Hey, how's the art history going? You ever find out why Reubens dug those fat broads? Not funny, right? Yeah, well, you never did have much of a sense of humour... Sure, I'm working. You think I just fart around all the time? I'm working my ass off, going like a tunnel digger. Plan on leaving this gold-plated hick town... At least before the market craps out. Yeah, I'm always leaving, so what. You think I wanna die in this sideshow of a city? It's not easy, tough to tie up the loose ends this place has. Besides, they're always telling you you're in New York or London or some super cosmopolis. You know what I mean. Toronto's strange in a way. You really start believing all this hype that you're somewhere until you get out of here. Then you realize you been nowhere at all. Yeah, I've heard this city's full to the eyeballs with opportunity, they been screaming it from the roof tops, the old three legged town has finally gotten on the map. Too bad it's got a blown colon... Maybe I should stick around and open a muzzle franchise, get into a little tasteful discipline, really clean up... Who? Oh yeah, I know them, so? Look, those two "creeps" are my friends. Is that right? Well, look at the sputtering eggheads you hang out with. Must be a laugh at parties. How about that whitebread journalist? The pork-eater you were stuck on. The guy who'd sing to you over the phone... Hey, wait, don't go...c'mon, I thought we were still friends...

I rush out after her, grab her by the elbow, can't believe this disloyalty. Her knuckles go up to her hips, one foot sticks out to the side slightly. She's about to put me through the blender when Stein and the Duke walk up. She stops, looks at them with a snort and throws her head sideways. "Here," she says to me, "the other two stooges." With that she turns and goes off.

They both stare after her, mouths open, hands in their pockets.

"What's with her?" asks Stein. "What'd we do?"

The Duke's snickering, his head in a rose coloured cloud. "Guess she can't handle the pressure, eh?"

Stein opens the door to the Cameron, peers through the stragglers, comes back sighing. "They're gettin flushed. What you guys wanna do?"

✳

Ten hours later I come-to on Stein's floor. I think I'm getting the hang of this. My brain fires through all chambers, blanks popping everywhere.

Stein's poking at me with the corner of a record jacket.

"Hey, Nick, get up."

"Huh?"

"Here," he says, pushing me with his foot. Bends over and hands me a cup of coffee. "Get off the floor."

Stein drags a couple ragged lawn chairs out of the house and sets them up in the driveway. It's two jobs getting to my feet, vertigo at the top of the back steps. Spastic joints hardly bending, the villain sun grinning from ear to ear again. Stein braces me as I focus on getting to the chair. Takes the coffee off me and leads me over. He lights a smoke, hands it to me and it's not long, not long enough before Chops comes flapping his feet up the drive. Sitting in the lawnchair it's like watching an experimental movie. This guy just coming and coming toward you, treadmilling up the pavement.

Chops is semi-pressed, wearing a light gray blazer, his hair is combed behind his ears. Stein notices Chops' feet, new loafers. "Nice creepers, Choparoonee. You gonna grow a moustache now?"

"I got a job," Chops answers, defensive.

"A job?" I'm fascinated. "What kinda job?"

"You know, a job where you show up everyday."

Stein's wide-eyed. "Well why aren't you riding the wheel right this minute?"

"I just got hired. I start on Monday."

"Ah...Monday," I say, "it's back to that, eh?"

"You guys are full of shit! At least I'll have some money for a change. Not be hung up on some prick's hook like you fuckers!"

"Listen to this," I growl, struggling to my feet. "You think you got somethin on us?"

"I never said I wanted nothin on you. You think I'm not in with you guys?"

"In what?" I shout. "You're not in anything at all, Chops. Fuck you, you teenybopper!"

Chops is getting baby mad, his mouth really wanting to say something. He's stealing looks at Stein as I slowly reach out for him. I feel Stein grab my arm.

"Don't bother, Nick."

Chops is shrinking by the second. Rapid melting down to a life like version of himself. He's moving off sideways, tears welling up. He turns away and leaves without a word, stops at the bottom of the drive and looks back. I shake my head, no.

29

Lacey gives me a clean shaven smirk. He passes every mirror without a glance. No need, he knows.

We're hunched over our table at the Rivoli. I'm in an out of the can doing a few lines, trying to chat up the waitress/model/actress/artist.

"I dunno why you like comin to this tourist trap," says Lace, swishing his drink around.

"Why not?" I reply. "I like lookin at the women."

"Women," he sneers. "These second rate clerks? Nick, you're a cheap sonofabitch."

"Yeah, I'm cheap. Keeps things on an even keel."

We're in a good way. It's early evening, middle of the week, no freak outs, but Lacey stares into me suddenly.

"Shank mentioned a problem with Chops," he says.

"Nothin," I answer. "Chops is nowhere, just lonely."

"You sure?"

"Don't worry," I tell him. "You really think anybody's interested in what happened to a guy like Mike? You think that nowadays somethin like that even matters?"

This relaxes Lace. He turns to signal for another round then looks back at me. "I guess you're right," he smiles. "There's a lot worse things in the world these days."

We wash down a few more bourbons and his Queen

Street meter is running low. "I gotta get off this drag," Lacey grouches. "It gives me the shits after an hour."

"Where to?" I ask.

He eyes me for a couple seconds, leaves a ten buck tip and goes toward the door.

30

~~~

Woken by the sound of a siren's howl, hungry through the night. Racing along wet streets, seeking bodies. Rabid ambulance driver jumps the curb to mow down any hapless loner.

Feeling in my bones a tube shoved down her throat in an overlit emergency ward. Hear her in a strangled sleep, calling out from the well.

We once had our clear quiet dawn rising very blue. Electric shade flattening out buildings, sounds. But she dripped out of one night or another, her fingers slipping from mine. Left me standing on the curb when the bars turned out and she got into a cab with another slick.

Never did get a chance to carve up our organs, the dumbest kind of sluts and she could hardly get off, could never really cum from me doing it as hard as I could.

But your little cunt is cold now. The stupid hole of yours that wouldn't explain itself. Your goddamn whining about how my dick didn't fit right. Peroxide, you just walked away. You walked away with your string lipped scowl and your idiot nickname. Those heels picking with sharp sounds at a thick night. In good faith you must have collapsed on an old couch to lie back and inhale your own vomit, teeth of the spike still at your

149

elbow. Where was your butcher shop mouth to open up and pour out a steaming rain, hissing and screeching just before dawn when I was begging for the light. You couldn't make the sky come down.

Now your nails will become long, sleek. Your skull will slowly smile and your roots will finally grow in. There's nothing stopping you, let me hear your footsteps near my bed. Any night at all, run to me. Don't stop to look both ways. Don't tie your hair back or put on lipstick or smell yourself to see if it's too much, that's all shut off now. Just run, I'll know it's you coming around.

Cold autumn rain will begin falling soon, I can feel the pollution thinning. I'll recognize the riff raff from their same old winter coats. I'll see your brand of cigarettes on the shelf in the corner grocer and hear your favourite music on the tape machines of the cooler clothing shops.

31

Guess the law of averages didn't work out. Cut down off the welfare rolls just cuz you picked up the phone. Price of beer and cigarettes going up, law and order campaign all over the place. Shut up, shut out and maybe it's time to really guess again. Stay well informed, keep the lies in some kind of order. Your own voice echoing back days later. Just one more shot at becoming a credible threat, thrown drunk out of every bar on the strip. Gather up these knees and move away, swearing revenge, rainwater ratsoaked. Griping to myself that every deranged slut has an opinion these days. Go for one more round of borrowed twenty dollar bills. *I'm good for it, you know that.*

Head down to the warehouse, find the Duke in his no plumbing cell. He's laid out with the Telecaster copy wired to a cracked radio speaker. Small cricket scrape of discord blues, a carpet of cigarette smoke about neck high.

The Duke looks eaten away, leftovers in the sink. He wandered this town for two decades telling everyone he met a different life story. Came over with the last boatload of white immigrants and has a long standing grudge. He's been trying to cash in on this place like any other aspiring ruler. Once, we used to practice for the big time. Going at it in Vic Memorial Square with garbage can lids and ax handles, though even that got bylawed away in time.

Always putting each other down out of ear shot as any good friends do. Living like pole sitters, spending the eternal morning over greasy eggs and ham. Always short of cash, long on time management. Talent scouts with a relentless work load, crippled by office politics. Yet, the Duke was always smarter in certain ways. He never took a ride out to a shag pad where the buses didn't run. Kept the sonar on in every potential land mine situation. Master of the high-speed orderly retreat, a regrouping expert and night combat legend. No, no dogs in his trees, he never got *his* sandwiches wet.

The Duke finally manages to cajole himself off the couch and get his socks on. We split a four hour old coffee and speculate as to Stein and his whereabouts. Haven't seen him around for awhile.

The guy just dropped out of sight, took the big plunge he was always threatening. A flying head-dive into middle class stardom with borrowed money, a clapped out '77 Pinto and a woman who claimed to love him.

Last time we saw Stein he'd shown up at Rooneem's wearing a moth eaten tweed blazer and carrying a bag of monkey wrenches.

"Lemme give yu a piece of advice," he'd told us. "Just get any kind a work, don't matter what. That's what I figured out. I can't live like you guys anymore, this time I mean it. I'll get a little wage job if I have to."

Stein had spent most of his life running away from his mother's house and now the door charge was steep. Had his eyeballs in hock till he could get his head above water. Went out and hired a daughter to keep his moorings straight. Rented a pad on the other side of town with his

152

girlfriend's pay cheque. Sewed a phone to his ear, collected partners like favourite quotes. Started busting down the door of every major megacorp in the yellow pages, showing them how it's done.

"You think it's funny?" he'd screamed at us. "Check out these shoes!" Pulled up his pant legs to show off black brogues.

"What did yu do?" the Duke'd scoffed at him. "Catch some board director sleepin it off in Nathan Philips Square?"

"If you wanna get jealous," Stein had humbly told us, "that's your problem. It's out there for everybody to take. Just go out an get it, that's my motto."

"Ok, then," I said, "how about my twenty bucks?"

That's when he got vindictive. "Yeah! Alright!" Went rummaging through his paint splattered bag and came up with a crisp, low mileage twenty.

"Here!" Stein yelled, as he'd slammed the bill onto the table. "Go on, you can have it! Cuttin into my cashflow. Businessmen never get a break these days. Nobody's got any faith, nobody..."

"It's a cold world," the Duke reminded him. "The first lesson of high finance."

Stein became infuriated, scarlet faced. Rocketed out of his chair and ran out in tears.

Me and the Duke just sat there staring at that twenty lying on the table. Somehow not surprised at all that Stein'd been pole-axed by a piece of paper with the Queen's head on it.

II

"That guy..." mutters the Duke, pulling on his shoes. "I guess he's really burned the clutch for good."

"Probably ended up in jail," I say. "Take a crash course in giving head."

"Smart thing to know," he agrees, getting to his feet. "A good mouth man can rise quickly in today's volatile markets. Anyway, Stein went nuts, who knows what happened to him. Who cares. Let's take a walk up to Shank's, see how the real empire's doing."

32

I hadn't seen much of Shank since my photo opportunity with Cheri. He'd been busy with a hair transplant and a new candidate he'd lured down from the suburbs.

Up at headquarters we find this team of workies buzzing around the house. Renovating, painting, picking the scales off the brick work with tooth brushes. Hardly recognize the old fort.

Go inside and it's been done over with pale greens and greys, white trim, this fussy wallpaper. All the heavy lounge gear is gone from the living room. Replaced with a dark wood desk, real delicate number, all set up like an office. Copies of GQ and Personal Finance on the tasteful coffee table. A couple wingbacks covered in Laura Ashley prints. There's this six-figure country club blonde sitting behind the desk, on the phone.

"Good afternoon, TorCan Investments, just a moment please." She presses the hold button and looks up at us. "May I help you?"

"Yeah, where's Shank?" I ask her.

"Pardon me?"

"Shank, the guy who lives here."

"May I inquire as to your business?"

"Our business?" asks the Duke. "You can tell him we brought the latest line in butt plugs."

Her lips sour, the eyes go half closed. "He's not in at the moment. I'm afraid he only works by appointment now."

"No shit?" I say. "Well, we got an appointment to install his new rectal guidance system."

The woman cracks a thin smile, clicks her blood red, manicured nails on the desk top. Annoyed, unthreatened, ready to call in the goons from outside. She looks past us thankfully and Lacey's at our shoulders, dressed, as usual, like a mortician. He nods at the receptionist and asks us to follow him into the kitchen. It's all been reworked heavy Braun, gleaming white, super function, a Kraut's idea of cozy.

"Fuck, Lace," I say, thumbing back at the blonde, "Shank's finally bought himself a little class, eh?"

"Here's the line," replies Lacey, not in the mood. "It's strictly legit from now on, no more bush league. Catherine in there is helping Shank run things by the book. Run things clean."

The Duke catches on, nods with approval, gazing around. "Sure, nice Chinese laundry..."

Lacey lets that explain. "Yeah, you got it. Image, right? It's just the way things are gonna be now. Gotta play it smart, you guys understand. But, if you two wanna clean up and wash yur socks," he adds, trying some compensation on us, "well...maybe a little work, employees, you know."

"Hold on a second," I tell him. "You fuckin joking? Don't gimme this employees bullshit. We're not those wage grunts out in the yard, man. What about the trick we turned with Cabbagetown Mike? I been carrying that around inside me, Lace."

His eyes freeze on me, go dark.

"You been carrying *what* around inside you, Nick?"

I look at the Duke, he's staring at the floor. A telephone

purrs from the other room. Shank's new piece answers it.

"Okay then," Lacey goes on, glancing at his watch. "right now, no hangin around. You guys gotta split."

We go down the hall past the living room. I stop in front of Catherine. Lacey tells me to move along as he steers us out the front door.

"See yu," he yells after us. "We'll have a drink soon and talk."

∞ ∞

I look back at the house as we're moving off.

"Christ, man, this is weird..."

"It was comin," says the Duke. "The party was gettin to be a drag."

"So what you gonna do?" I ask him.

The Duke doesn't hear my question, his mind already elsewhere. He's feeling his stubble, checking his hair in a car window. Looks down at the has-been body and tucks in his ripped shirt tail. Takes out a few small crumpled bills, flattens them neatly, folds them in order and slips them into his pocket.

We walk back down to Queen without saying much and he gets rid of me at the corner of Bathurst.

"I gotta few things to do," he says, looking off. "I'll see you around."

I watch him walk away southward. It's late afternoon, everyone's getting off work, going home.

Basil Papadimos was born in Toronto, 1957. His short ficton has appeared in *LIES*. *Magazine*, *UnWorld Quarterly* and *Magnetic City News*. He has written and produced a number of low budget videotapes including *The Life of Dinosaurs During the Recession*, winner of the 1986 Benthouse LPV Award. ***The Hook Of It Is*** is his first novel. He currently lives in Montréal.